HOW TO CHOOSE A HUSBAND

a very large print later-in-life romantic comedy set in a Cotswold village

Stefania Hartley

The Sicilian Mama

ALSO AVAILABLE AS EBOOK AND SMALLER FONT PAPERBACK

ISBN: 978-1-914606-57-1

This title was first published as a pocket novel by The People's Friend.

Edited by Sandy Salisbury

Cover illustration and design by Joseph Witchall

https://josephwitchall.com/

CHAPTER 1

"Good men are like nuggets of gold—and more precious still.

But the chances of finding them among the rocks are almost nil."

—From The Sicilian Mama's "How to Pick a Husband" blog.

Grazia Colonna had waited fifty years to meet The One. There had been a few false alarms along the way, but this time she felt it could be her chance.

She turned in her hands the thick, glossy white card that invited her to her friend's wedding this weekend. Rebecca had told her that there would be many eligible bachelors at her wedding and, as she was getting married for the second time, she should know a thing or two, Grazia felt. Whoever may be the Powers Above who held the strings of the purse of love, He/She/They must have realised that Grazia Colonna had waited long enough.

Her mother walked into her room —without knocking, as usual.

"Why are you staring at that invitation?"

Grazia closed the card and put it down on her desk. "Just checking the date."

"It's on Saturday."

Grazia wished her mother hadn't been invited too.

"I hope you've chosen your dress," Rosaria said.

"I was just about to."

Rosaria clicked her tongue. "Lazy, last-minute girl."

Her mother was wrong. It was

neither laziness nor procrastination, and certainly not brinkmanship, but fear. The wrong outfit—too prudish or too revealing, too dark (mourning her friend) or too light (aspiring bride)—could put off The One.

Rosaria rolled her eyes and left the room.

Grazia opened her cupboard and reviewed her smart clothes. She could do with something new for the occasion, but right now there was no money for that.

The skirt and blouse she'd worn for her father's funeral were definitely too dark. She tried putting on the dress she'd worn at her cousin's wedding, twenty years ago. No hope of squeezing into this one, nor into the dress she'd worn at her niece's First Holy Communion back in Italy. All these clothes were from aeons ago and when Grazia had been many kilos lighter!

She picked the white and purple flowery dress she'd worn at her British citizenship ceremony. This was a lot more recent.

She removed her blouse and skirt, sucked in her tummy, stepped into the dress and pulled. It got stuck at her hips. She tried wriggling into it from underneath but it got stuck at her shoulders.

Her two options were losing weight or altering the dress. She was about to open a delicatessen with her mother, so option one was out of the question.

Could the dress be made larger? She checked the seams. A few centimetres on each side, just about enough to fit her, but certainly with no margin for error. Dare she attempt the alteration herself?

She glanced at her sewing machine on the floor. No, she could not. This was the dress for the day she might meet The One.

If she moved the seam too close to the fabric's fraying edges, the dress could rip open during the meal. If she was too cautious and didn't move the seam far enough, the dress wouldn't fit her, even before the meal.

This was a job that required the utmost precision. One for the professionals.

The town's seamstress! Grazia had seen the shop on the high street but hadn't been inside. She hoped it wasn't a snooty place for country ladies who wanted their tweeds and jodhpurs made to measure.

Grazia's choices were the seamstress or her mother. She trusted her mother's sewing skills more than her own but her kindness much less: Rosaria was likely to tell her to lose weight instead. She would insist that no man would look at her in her current state, or something to that effect. No, her mother did not need more ammunition to berate her with.

Grazia folded the dress carefully into a clean bag, checked that Rosaria was snoozing in her room, then closed the door of the flat carefully behind her.

CHAPTER 2

The high street bustled with antiques shops and jewellers, fancy restaurants and florists. Nothing actually useful, except for the seamstress's shop.

Grazia imagined her as a buxom lady with a silver chignon and a kindly smile—just like she conjured up the Sicilian Mama of the "How to Pick a Husband" blog.

She would be at her sewing machine, making a pretty dress for a little girl or sewing a button eye on a poorly teddy. She would examine Grazia's dress and say, "What a lovely dress, dear. I'll fix it and you'll look fabulous at your friend's wedding."

At the touch of her fairy godmother wand she'd turn the dress into a sparkly evening gown complete with glass slippers and gloves, all the while singing a catchy tune.

"Mark my words," she would say,

"this is the last wedding you'll attend that isn't your own. And no, you're not a monster for feeling a teensy bit envious of your friend. You're absolutely normal. Now, sit down and have a cup of tea."

Grazia had reached the barber's shop before she realised she had passed the wattle-and-daub building. She turned around and walked back.

Two headless mannequins in suits guarded the door. With pins stuck into their pockets and lapels and their woeful lack of heads, they looked less like soldiers and more like cautionary tales for potential trespassers.

Grazia glanced at the windows, half-expecting to see their severed heads impaled on spears. Instead, there were only bolts of tartan and tweed.

She pushed the door and stepped in. The rat-tat-tat-tat of a sewing machine drowned the jangle of the doorbell and carried on.

Inside, the place was dark, dingy and dusty. No pink tulle, flowery silks or red and white gingham. This was a kingdom of greys, navys and browns.

Spiky pin cushions, enormous scissors and fierce-looking steam irons were dotted around the place, and the carcass of a whole roast chicken sat on a plate, picked clean—the seamstress's lunch? Rather than the dwelling of a fairy godmother, this place seemed like somewhere Hansel and Gretel would have found the witch. Well, if this seamstress was no fairy godmother but a witch, so be it. Grazia wouldn't be the first human in history to turn to a witch for help in the pursuit of love.

Guided by the rattle, she made her way through the maze of clothes racks and reached the sewing machine.

Not a witch. A wizard.

A man of about her own age was stooped over a beautiful vintage Singer sewing machine. A pair of spectacles were perched on his nose, another pair sat on his head like a halo, and two more dangled around his neck. He was adorned with spectacles, or maybe it was just his way of coping with the room's poor lighting.

"Hello. I've come to see the seamstress." Grazia bellowed over the noise of the machine.

The man carried on sewing without looking up. Might he be watching her through those glasses on the top of his head?

"The tailor, you mean." The deep rumble of his voice was in step with the rhythm of the machine.

"Actually, no, I need a seamstress. Is there one here?"

A colleague, an assistant, a witch-in-residence. Anyone but you, she thought.

"Why a seamstress?"

"I need a dress altered."

"That's what tailors do."

The rattle of the machine stopped and the man finally looked up. He had light blue eyes. Magnified by the spectacles, they were enormous, but even over the reading glasses they were big.

"Yes, to men's clothes."

"No. Any clothes. Hence the word 'tailoring'."

Was he trying to teach her English? Did he think that, just because she had a foreign accent, she didn't know the language?

She raised her chin, ready to retort that she knew very well the difference between a tailor and a seamstress. Then she realised that she didn't! The truth was that she needed a woman because there was no way she wanted a strange male draping, pinching and smoothing fabric over her body.

"Can I see the garment?"

He stretched out a hand. How could such a large hand possibly thread a needle?

"I've changed my mind," she stammered. "Thanks and goodbye."

Grazia made to turn around and leave, but then he spoke.

"The nearest seamstress is in Swindon."

CHAPTER 3

Oh, no. With no car and possibly several appointments for fitting, Swindon wasn't an option.

Reluctantly, Grazia pulled the purple dress from her bag. "I need it enlarged," she said awkwardly.

The tailor switched to a different

pair of glasses and inspected the dress. "It's not always possible to move seams out."

"I know, but I've already checked and there's enough fabric."

"That depends on how much you want it let out."

"Enough to fit me."

He ran a measuring gaze over her and she squirmed. This was why she had wanted a seamstress.

"To fit you now or in the future?" he asked.

"What do you mean?"

"People always mean to lose weight in the future. Usually that doesn't happen."

"To fit me now."

He nodded. "Good. We could gain a couple of centimetres out of each seam, but it will all need unstitching and restitching. It's not going to be an easy job."

"Do what's needed. So long as the dress doesn't burst open when I sit down or eat."

He pursed his lips. "That would never happen to something I've sewn."

He wasn't going to give the job to a female assistant, then. She could still say no and leave, but first she must recover her dress. “You won’t be able to do it before this Saturday.” It was a statement, not a question.

“I will.”

“I don’t want a rushed job. I want it done properly.”

He straightened his back. “I always do my job properly.”

“I mean, with extra care. Otherwise I could do it myself.”

“Why don’t you, then?”

“Because I don’t want to risk it.”

“Everything is a risk. Life itself is the ultimate risk—of death. You’re risking less by letting me alter your dress than by doing it yourself.” He gave a small smile. "Plus, if anything goes wrong, you can blame me instead of yourself."

That was definitely a bonus. Also, he'd done a very neat job on the trouser zipper he had just sewn. It would be silly to refuse him the job. "Fine. How much will it be?"

He turned the dress inside out and examined it again, exposing all the seams. She felt like she was the one to be turned inside out and examined. She inched towards the door. Fresh light streamed in from outside.

"Twenty pounds. Payment on

delivery."

"Fine. Goodbye."

"Wait."

He got up from his chair and the spectacles on the top of his head skimmed the ceiling. Ah, that was what they were for: a safety helmet.

He ducked under an exposed beam without looking, then disappeared through some racks and reappeared behind the till. He picked up a receipt book and a pen.

"Name?" he asked.

"Why should I give you my name?"

"For the collection ticket."

She sighed. She hated her name

and hated giving it to people. In Britain it gave her away as a foreigner—if her accent hadn't already—and most people didn't know how to spell it. In Italy she didn't have these problems, but everyone there knew that "Disgrazia"—what her mother actually called her day-to-day—meant 'misfortune'.

Right there was an extra problem. If Grazia gave the tailor her name, Rosaria might find out that she'd been at his shop.

"Grace," she answered. It was close enough.

"Telephone number?"

"I don't have a phone."

He frowned. "I may need to contact you if I have questions about the dress."

"I'll drop by regularly."

"As you wish. Now, get undressed in that cubicle and I'll take your measurements." She must have looked horrified, because he added, "Just down to your blouse."

That was better, but she knew he would be running a measuring tape around her waist, hips and... chest! This was why she had wanted a seamstress instead of a tailor.

"I will measure myself at home and

phone in the numbers."

"So you do have a phone?" The tailor hid a smile. "As you wish. Only, if you give me the measurements, then you take responsibility for any inaccuracies."

"There won't be any inaccuracies."

"So long as we know where we stand."

She knew very well where she stood—too far from the door. She took the collection receipt and all but ran out of the shop.

CHAPTER 4

Grazia walked briskly past the antiques shops, the florists and the jewellers, the restaurants and the teashops, with her eyes fixed on the pavement and her cheeks aflame.

How had she got herself into a situation where a man had asked her to undress, unchaperoned, in the back of his shop?

When she got home, her mother was still napping. Good. Grazia washed her hands and splashed her face with cold water, then took her sewing box out of the cupboard and found the measuring tape.

The tailor needed her bust, waist and hip size. Nothing would be left to the imagination. She sighed and wrapped the measuring tape around her body, scratching the numbers on a piece of paper with a pencil stub. Then she picked up her phone and rang the number on the collection ticket.

"Hector Gonzales, tailor."

Gonzales? The tailor was Spanish?

"Hello?" he repeated.

"This is Graz—ahem, Grace," she whispered so as not to wake her mother.

"Hello, Grace."

"I have the measurements for you."

"Great. I'll just grab pen and paper."

Oh, no. This was likely to take some time. Her first impression of the shop had been of unbridled mess. It might be easier to find a needle in a haystack than in this shop.

Down the phone came the heavy thud of a roll of fabric, the rustling of paper, the opening and closing of wooden drawers. If he couldn't find a pen, he'd have to memorise her measurements until he found something to write with. What if he forgot them?

"Ready," he announced.

"Okay. Hips..."

"Who are you talking to?" Rosaria interrupted from the threshold in Italian.

Grazia hung up hurriedly and pocketed the phone. Her mother had this awful habit of sneaking up on people. Next Christmas Grazia might get her some wooden clogs to wear at home. "Nobody. You're already up, I see."

"I don't sleep in the afternoon. You know that," Rosaria retorted.

But a pair of hairclips had migrated from her temples to the top of her head, her dark little eyes were pinheads and her black skirt and black blouse were crumpled. Still, Rosaria would never admit to succumbing to an afternoon siesta because the devil found work for idle hands, and sloth was one of the seven deadly sins. However, age and Italian genes usually overcame the old woman's willpower. Grazia had proof of that—unless the noises coming from Rosaria's bedroom between two and four in the afternoon were from a gentle vacuum cleaner.

Rosaria's eyes narrowed in on the measuring tape in Grazia's hands. "What's that tape for?"

"Nothing."

"Who were you talking to?"

She stepped into the room, blocking Grazia's exit. Her mother had canine levels of persistence.

Despite being the offspring of two egregiously pig-headed people,

Grazia hadn't inherited a drop of this trait. It was as if a donkey had mated with a mule and they had produced a chicken. Grazia was a genetic outlier. This made her no match for her mother and, unfortunately, both of them knew it.

At this point, trying to shake her mother off was impossible. Rosaria had all the time, inclination and desire to grind Grazia down until she answered her question. Lying was no option either. Rosaria would interrogate her until Grazia had tangled herself up completely. Grazia had no choice but to tell the truth.

"It was the town's tailor."

"You went to a tailor's shop?"

Her mother spoke as though a tailor's shop were a den of iniquity.

"I needed help with a dress. It was too delicate a job," Grazia muttered.

Rosaria sniffed. "Too delicate for you, perhaps, but surely not for me. What is it that you need to do?"

"Make it larger," Grazia whispered even though, right now, she felt anything but large.

"You should lose weight instead of making dresses larger."

Just as Grazia had predicted. "There isn't enough time. I need it for

Rebecca's wedding."

"Let's see this dress."

Rosaria marched to Grazia's wardrobe and yanked it open. She flicked through her daughter's clothes with the disapproving expression of someone leafing through the pages of an insufferably boring book.

"It's not here. It's at the tailor's," Grazia said.

"Then, you have to get it back immediately! That man is not touching it. Have you already paid?"

"No."

"Go and get it back, then."

"What if he's already started on it?"

"If he has, it means that he hasn't got enough customers, which is a bad sign. Go!"

Dread lodged itself in the pit of Grazia's stomach. The last thing she wanted was her mother altering her dress. Not only would she do it carelessly and the seams might come undone, but she would also comment on Grazia's body all through the sewing and the fittings. This was a disaster. The dress in which she was going to meet The One mustn't be tainted by bad feelings.

But Grazia's lips couldn't form the word "no". In all of her fifty years, they never had.

CHAPTER 5

"'Till death do us part' was invented

When people died young and were easily contented."

—From The Sicilian Mama's "How to Pick a Husband" blog.

As she retraced her steps to the tailor's dingy den, Grazia kept her eyes pinned to the ground. From the opposite pavement, from inside the shops and from the windows of their homes, people must be judging her, she felt.

Some would disapprove of her letting her mother boss her around. Others would tut-tut about her going to the tailor in the first place, when she had already known that her mother wouldn't like it. People who wanted to judge always found a reason.

When her friend, Rebecca, mother of three boys, had left her first husband, some had judged her for leaving a husband of fifteen years who hadn't done anything wrong. Others had judged her for staying for fifteen years with a husband who hadn't done anything right!

One day Rebecca had had enough of carrying the whole weight of the family on her shoulders. Of feeling alone even when he was with her. She told him goodbye.

After all, "till death do us part" had been invented when people died in their forties, which was exactly Rebecca's age when she had walked out on Kev. As she entered her "bonus" life, it seemed like Rebecca had needed a bonus husband too.

Maybe Grazia wasn't too late in finding love after all.

***

The tailor's door chime jangled into a silent shop. All you could hear was the creaking of floorboards in the flat upstairs. There wasn't anyone at the sewing machine nor at the till.

Grazia spotted a picture of a woman on the wall. She hadn't noticed her the first time. The woman had dark hair and glasses. Could there be a seamstress working in the shop after all?

Grazia walked up to the counter

and leaned forward to study the photo. The woman had the expression of someone who was contented with her life. Under the photo was a name: *Fiona Gonzales*. The tailor's wife, then? There were two dates below the photo. Oh, dear, the woman was dead!

This complicated matters. How could she take the job away from a sad, bereaved man?

The trouble was that her mother surely wouldn't let it drop.

"I'm at the back!" the tailor called.

Grazia jumped and looked around. Had he seen her staring at the photo?

"In the room at the back!" he called again.

She followed the direction of the voice. The room was behind a wattle-and-daub wall. Through a diamond-leaded window natural light streamed onto a large, uncluttered table like sunlight through a clearing in a forest. Stretched over the table was Grazia's dress—or, rather, the parts of it. Her ribcage squeezed.

"You've already started!"

He must have taken her words as praise instead of an acknowledgement of the damage, because he smiled.

"Yes. I've prioritised this job, given the time constraint." Then he looked up at her and his smile drained. "Is everything all right?"

"No. Yes. No!" she stammered.

Even if she paid for the work the tailor had already done, it would feel cold-hearted to take the job from him after his kindness. "I'm just not used to seeing my dress broken down to its body parts," she answered, which was also true.

The dress reminded her of a dissected frog in a science lesson. She just hoped that it could be put back together and still be wearable.

The tailor shrugged. "I would never have shown you this stage of the work under normal circumstances. I've been expecting you to ring back with your measurements."

Ah, the measurements. "Sorry, I left the paper at home."

Because she had only come to take the dress back. Now that she wasn't going to do that, what was she going to tell her mother?

If Grazia told her the truth, Rosaria was perfectly capable of storming into the shop and demanding the dress back from the tailor.

Wait a moment. She had never told her mother which dress she was getting altered. She could give Rosaria any of the dresses in her cupboard! It was at moments like this that she believed that God existed and loved humankind.

"Never mind about the measurements. If you wait a few minutes, I'll baste the dress and I can fit it directly on you," the tailor offered.

Grazia considered. As she was weighing up whether or not this option was better than rushing home and risking being intercepted by her mother, a door opened somewhere upstairs.

Excited young voices and quick steps rumbled down the stairs at the back of the shop. One, two, three girls from early to late teens, all unmistakably related to the tailor, tumbled into the shop.

"I'm working," he told them gruffly.

"We just need some money for ice cream," the oldest girl begged.

She had wonderful eyelashes and beautiful eyes. She turned to Grazia with a smile. "Hello."

"Hello," Grazia replied, slightly

mesmerized.

"Where are you going?" the tailor asked his daughters.

"To the cinema, Dad," the middle girl said. "We told you yesterday."

She had a studded collar and piercings on her lips and nose. She noticed Grazia's dress on the worktable and turned back to the tailor. " Finally something different to sink your teeth into!"

The metaphor gave Grazia goosebumps.

The tailor rocked on his stool, retrieved his wallet from a back pocket and handed Eyelashes Girl a

£20 note.

"That's not enough—the food is expensive there," Collar Girl protested.

He handed over another note.

"We're not just after your money, Daddy, honest," the youngest said.

She wrapped her arms around her father's shoulders and kissed him lovingly on the one spot on his head that was free from spectacles.

"Bring back the change!" he called after them.

But they were already through the door and gone.

CHAPTER 6

Once his daughters had left, the tailor turned to Grazia. "Sorry about that."

He probably expected her to respond with something like, "I know. Kids are all the same!"

She didn't. People often assumed that she had experience of children, either from her own or through family members. The trouble was that she had missed the boat regarding parenthood. In addition, her own childhood had been so different from most people's that she didn't know what was normal and what wasn't. So she usually didn't say anything.

In this case, she decided she could speak. She knew that the tailor's daughters had lost their mother, after all, and that must count for a lot.

"Well, poor things, they've lost their mum."

Storm clouds instantly swept over his face and the temperature in the room plummeted.

"The girls are fine," he growled.

Oh, no, she had upset him! Why couldn't she ever say anything right?

"Of course. I'm sure you're a great father and, being a tailor, you must know that belts are for holding trousers up, not for beating children," she gabbled.

"I'll start basting," he interrupted.

"Sure."

He offered her a stool to sit on, handed over a copy of "Vogue" and went off to fetch his needles and threads.

Still reeling from her faux pas, Grazia flicked through the pages without seeing them. She had really put her foot in it and upset him. Silly woman.

He returned and hitched himself up onto the table, sat cross-legged with the garment resting on his lap and started sewing.

The traditional tailor's posture! Grazia had seen it in black-and-white photos of tailors from the past, but this was the first time in real life. She did a little jump on her stool.

"Did you know that, because of

the tailor's habit of sitting cross-legged, one muscle of the leg is named 'sartorius', the tailor's muscle?" she asked, finding the silence uncomfortable. "It's the longest muscle in the body and goes from the outside of the hip to the inside of the knee in a very elegant curve," she finished.

He glanced at her over his glasses and handed her a different magazine. "If you're bored."

Grazia was far from bored, but she opened the new magazine obediently and pretended to read while she carried on watching him.

Needle and thread had disappeared inside his hand, and his fingers skimmed gracefully over the fabric. Even in the trickiest corners, like around the zipper and the armpits, the fabric seemed to surrender to his hands. Whenever he needed to fix the thread, he only had to rub his fingers together and a knot appeared as if by magic.

She noticed his wedding ring. She had reached the age when this was usually the first thing she noticed on men, but she hadn't this time.

How sweet and sad that he still wore it. She found herself imagining his hands caressing his wife's cheeks with the same gentleness with which he was handling the fabric.

He looked up and caught her watching him. She flushed and pinned her gaze on the magazine page that had been open on her lap for the past five minutes. It was a double-page photo of a handsome male model. She flicked to another page and stared vacantly at luxury watches, trying to banish images from her mind. The tailor's skilful hands caressing the fabric of her dress. His big blue eyes, magnified by the glasses. His sartorius muscle—

that long, long muscle running down the thigh until just below the knee.

"Almost finished," he said suddenly.

She flushed as if she had been caught doing something she shouldn't. "The stitches are too wide," she protested defensively.

He raised an eyebrow. "They're just basting stitches."

"They're too close to the edge. The fabric will fray."

"It won't. I'll finish the edges later."

"How is that possible? There isn't enough fabric for pinking shears or an overlocker finish."

He stopped sewing and pinned her with his gaze. His silver thimble glinted. "I was under the impression that I was the tailor here."

"Yes, you are, but I'm the customer and the customer is always right."

Surprisingly, sweet dimples formed on his cheeks. He resumed working and his next stitches were a lot shorter.

"Here you go. You can try it on in the changing room."

In Grazia's world shops fell into two categories: those that had changing rooms with doors, and those with curtains only.

Whoever had decided that curtains were appropriate screens for changing rooms was either a voyeur or a sadist. Possibly both. There were so many ways for curtains to let one down. Gusts of wind, though improbable, were not impossible. Backlighting could turn changing rooms into shadow theatres.

Curtains never, ever reached the edges of the cubicle. To make matters worse, the cubicle was never spacious enough to position yourself out of the line of sight of the chink in the curtain.

The coup de grâce was the mirror. Useless for looking at yourself as it was far too close, it was extremely effective at multiplying the field of view of any person outside.

CHAPTER 7

To Grazia's dismay the tailor's changing room was a curtained one. In addition, as it was situated under the stairs, it comprised a sloping ceiling and a triangular opening. The curtain wasn't even attempting to reach the corners.

"I'll just clear this up for you." The tailor grabbed a pile of magazines from the floor, which at present were helpfully plugging the corner the curtain didn't reach. He was making the situation a lot worse.

"I don't use changing rooms with curtains," Grazia told him boldly.

He hovered with the pile of magazines in his arms until, unable to find any other free surface, he put them back where they had been before. "Would you like to use the bathroom upstairs instead?"

She blinked. "It's improper for a woman to get undressed in a man's flat."

"It's also my daughters' flat," he pointed out.

"But they're not here."

He scratched his cheeks pensively. "Well, how about I go upstairs while you get changed here on your own?"

She considered this. "That will do, thank you."

He handed her the dress and plodded up the stairs.

Grazia tugged at the curtain four times before accepting that the fabric hoops wouldn't slide any further on the wooden beam without a chance she'd be pulling the whole thing down.

She checked the gaps on the sides. If someone stood between the till and the sewing machine, they would be able to see her reflected in the mirror. She stepped out of that line of sight. Now she was only exposed from the other side, but the onlooker would have to be sitting on the worktable, which was an unlikely scenario.

She removed her blouse and skirt and was about to step into the dress when she caught herself in the mirror. The brutally close mirror.

There was the scar on her knees

from back when she was still a child in Italy. Afraid of being left behind by her cousins, she had ridden her bike too fast along a gravel road. Higher up, on her thigh, was the scar from when she'd been bitten by the neighbours' dog. She had been afraid of dogs ever since.

The doorbell jangled and Grazia froze. Someone had entered the shop, and here she was, covered only by her grey underwear and her scars. She hopped into her dress.

"Mr Gonzales?" It was the voice of an elderly man.

Should she call out something to

send him away or pretend she wasn't there? In either case, being dressed would help a lot.

She yanked the dress up her legs too quickly and it stuck at her hips. Calm down, she scolded herself.

"Mr Gonzales, are you hiding from me?" the man shouted imperiously.

He had either a walking stick or a wooden leg he liked to clump on the floor like a seventeenth-century pirate. The thumping was getting closer to where she hid.

Grazia yanked the dress up again, but the panic sweat on her bare skin wasn't helping at all.

Heavy steps came thundering down the stairs.

"Lord Oldwell, hello!" she heard the tailor exclaim.

She was saved!

"I wasn't expecting you until tomorrow," he continued.

"I was passing by and I thought I'd save myself a trip."

"I'm sorry, but I'm busy with another client."

Grazia spied on the two men through the chink in the curtain. The tailor was ushering the elderly gentleman firmly away from the changing room. She let out a breath.

"Where's this other client of yours? I don't see anyone."

"In the changing room."

"It's Littleton, isn't it? That rascal has asked you to make the same suit for him, hasn't he?"

"No, he hasn't, I assure you."

"I don't believe you. Come out of hiding, you coward!"

The old man swivelled on his stick and made to go back towards the changing cubicle.

Grazia stifled a whimper and hunkered behind the magazines, still only half-dressed. If she was ever going to expire from a heart attack, it would be at this moment, she thought.

The tailor stepped in front of the old man, blocking his way. "It's not the Earl of Littleton, your Lordship. It's someone else."

Was he reluctant to say that she was a woman?

"Humph! Well, if that old maggot asks you to copy my suit, don't do it. He has already pinched a hound that I wanted and that nincompoop doesn't even hunt! The old coot is just hell-bent on upsetting me."

"I certainly won't," Mr Gonzales assured him. "Come back tomorrow and your suit will be ready for you."

The tailor's tone was gentle but firm, and the noise of the walking stick receded. The door jangled and all was silent again except inside Grazia's chest.

Gentler steps approached her cubicle.

"Sorry about that. Are you okay?" the tailor asked her in a low whisper. He had a very comforting voice.

"Yes."

"I've locked the door now and I'm going back upstairs."

"No, please, stay."

"Okay."

Through the mirror she watched him sit on a stool, facing away from her like a guard. She felt a lot better.

She took a couple of long, steadying breaths and tried again to pull her dress up, but more gently this time. The dress complied.

Despite the lack of measurements, the size was perfect. The tailor must have estimated it correctly just by looking at her.

The thought sent a frisson up Grazia's back. The only men who paid attention to her body were doctors and, for them, bodies were just heaps of flesh, cartilage, and bones.

Problems to fix.

What were bodies for tailors, though? Soft mannequins? Problems to hide? Perhaps even gifts to wrap?

She ran her hands over her hips to smooth the fabric. Sometimes, she thought, the wrapping was nicer than the gift.

CHAPTER 8

She opened the curtain and stepped out of the changing room. The tailor turned around and scanned her dress with an appraising eye. Now Grazia knew how tailors saw bodies: they were clothes-fillers.

Armed with a pin cushion on each wrist, a measuring tape whipped around his neck and his collection of spectacles hanging over his waistcoat, Hector Gonzales looked like a warrior ready for battle.

He pushed a stool in front of her. "Could you step up, please?"

She climbed onto the stool. If she imagined being a Greek statue on a plinth, she'd be fine. She must channel her inner Aphrodite.

He paced around her, studying the dress. She sucked in her tummy.

"You can breathe normally," he said.

She let her tummy out.

"I reckon we could bring it in

a little at the shoulders here." He pulled the fabric at her shoulder with feather-light touch.

The nape of her neck broke into goosebumps.

"We could take some off here, too." He pinched a little fabric at her waist and more goosebumps broke out all over her body. Channel your inner mannequin, she urged herself.

"Now it's perfect." He ran a hand over her hips, smoothing the fabric.

A dizzy mannequin...

"Can you lift your hair up, please?" he asked from behind her.

She couldn't. The nape of her neck

was covered in goosebumps. She pretended she hadn't heard and he started working on the zipper on her back through her hair.

"We might have to let out some fabric on the sides to ease the chest area."

"The chest area is perfectly fine," she argued hastily to prevent him touching the fabric in that embarrassing area.

He scratched his chin. "Okay. Perhaps we could add fabric inserts to make it more comfortable for you."

Comfortable wasn't a word Grazia

would ever associate with this dress again. Thankfully, he stepped away and walked over to the shelves where the bolts of fabric were stacked. Now that he had exited her personal space, Grazia felt herself breathe and expand again.

He returned with a beautiful, black silk satin. It captured the light and bounced it back enriched with an extra dose of elegance.

"I could use this fabric for the inserts." He offered her the bolt to touch and she ran her fingertips over its smooth silkiness. It must be the stuff tuxedo lapels and dinner bow ties were made from.

"It would echo the black edging of the flower petals and draw attention to the shape of the body," the tailor explained.

"This body doesn't want attention!"

"I mean, it would contour it. I can baste it on and show it to you, then you can decide if you like it."

"Well, okay."

He opened a drawer and pulled out a seam ripper. Was he going to rip the dress open while she was still inside it?

He must have seen the worry in her

eyes.

"You can get back into your clothes. I'll play around with the inserts and I'll telephone you when the dress is ready for another fitting."

"Don't."

He might call her while she was within her mother's earshot.

"Is another fitting absolutely necessary?"

If it was going to be anything like this one, Grazia's heart might not take it.

"Yes. If coming to the shop is difficult, then for an extra charge I do home visits, too."

"No! I mean, no, thank you. I'll pop round regularly."

"As you wish. If you come back tomorrow after lunch, the dress should be ready for a fitting."

Grazia left the shop. Before stepping out into the street, she looked left and right, like a criminal checking that the coast is clear. After her first visit to the tailor, she had felt a little guilty, but now she felt ready for the noose! She had disobeyed her mother, harboured illicit thoughts and felt things she shouldn't feel.

She walked briskly home, planning which dress she'd sacrifice to her mother. She would have to be quick if she didn't want to be seen returning from the tailor's empty-handed.

Her mobile phone vibrated in her pocket. One missed call and a voice message from Rebecca. She would listen to it later.

CHAPTER 9

"What's in an age? A man who's sixty years old

At any other age would still be brass if he's brass, and gold if he's gold."

—From The Sicilian Mama's "How to Pick a Husband" blog.

Grazia stared at the text message in dismay. Rebecca had been delayed in Rome by a volcanic eruption that had spewed ash into the sky and grounded all flights. Unless she found another way to get home on time, she would miss her own wedding.

Postponing the wedding would be a big inconvenience for Rebecca, but a catastrophe for her friend. If the wedding was put off, then The One might lose his way again. After waiting for him for fifty years, Grazia had concluded that he was prone to disorientation.

How much longer would she then have to wait before he finally landed at her harbour? At their age there were no guarantees he'd ever make it.

Rebecca's news had rattled Grazia so much that, for the very first time, she had posted a comment on the Sicilian Mama's blog:

"Is fifty years old too late to find The One?"

The Sicilian Mama answered immediately. "It's never too late, my love. Hang in there."

There was an old Sicilian folk song about a daughter asking her mum to find her a husband, because helping others find The One was a job for a Sicilian Mama.

But when Grazia had turned off her laptop and tried to sleep, the Mama's optimism had vanished with the light of her bedside lamp. Doubts had crept out again like monsters hiding under her sad, single bed.

No, Rebecca was going to make it on time. She was the kind of woman who knew what she wanted and took it. It had been that way since their schooldays in London, when Grazia had just arrived from Italy. Rebecca would get to her wedding even if she had to swim across the Channel.

It was a shame she wouldn't be there for the deli's opening tomorrow, though.

***

Grazia lifted a 25-litre drum of olive oil onto the shop counter and started pouring it into the pretty glass jars Rebecca had sourced from a local artisan.

"Your friend has abandoned us," Rosaria said sourly, slapping mozzarella plaits into a bowl of water.

Opening another Italian food outlet had been far from Grazia's intention, but Rebecca had been adamant that Calcotbury's high street was crying out for an Italian delicatessen. She had secured a favourable rental price for these premises, just a couple of shops down from her own antiques shop.

Rosaria had been very keen but, if the business didn't take off, Grazia knew that her mother would blame Rebecca.

"It's not Rebecca's fault that the volcano erupted," Grazia argued.

"Your friend has abandoned us just when we need her protection!"

Rosaria picked up a salami and pushed it hard through the rotary slicer.

"We don't need protection."

"Really? Like we didn't need it when our restaurant...?"

Rosaria didn't finish the sentence. What had happened to their restaurant could never be mentioned. But she also made sure that it could never be forgotten.

Through the shop's window, Grazia spotted the Italian wholesaler's van, the driver looking lost. She rushed outside and flagged it down. As the driver started reversing into the unloading bay, the wine shop's van swerved carelessly around it. A drunk driver?

The postman took advantage of the momentary obstruction in the traffic to stop his van in the middle of the road in order to complete a couple of deliveries, before jumping back in as soon as the traffic started moving again.

Grazia guided the wholesaler's driver to the back of the shop. All the refrigerated goods would go into the walk-in fridge at the back of the shop until the electrician had fixed the refrigerated display counter. Hopefully that would be this afternoon.

Grazia told herself not to panic. Rosaria had refused to do a launch party so, if the display counters weren't repaired in time, they could put off their official opening by a day or two depending on the expiry date of the mozzarellas.

At the sight of the piles of boxes to unpack, Rosaria announced that she had developed a sudden headache. Abandoning the part-sliced salami, the disarranged mozzarellas and her daughter, she disappeared upstairs.

Grazia inspected the consignment, checked every item against the delivery note and signed off the paperwork. Then she proceeded to unpack the boxes.

CHAPTER 10

The door chimed and a man walked in, ignoring the "Closed" sign.

Dressed in a green tweed jacket and salmon-pink trousers, he didn't look like a tradesman or delivery man, even for Calcotbury.

"Hello! I'm Rupert Brown and I

own the antiques shop right next door. Welcome to Calcotbury."

He had salt-and-pepper hair, a whippet-like face and, Grazia saw, no wedding ring.

"Nice to meet you."

She pulled her hands out of the mozzarella bowl and wiped them on her apron so that she could offer him one. But he didn't offer his hand so she pulled hers away.

He glanced at her apron, which had the words "Rosaria's Pantry" embroidered on it.

"You must be Rosaria."

"No, I'm her daughter, Grace."

"Hello, Grace, and welcome to our town. How do you find Calcotbury?"

This sounded like the beginning of one of those inane conversations that are the necessary first step in a new acquaintance. She found them fiendishly difficult to navigate because the truth was rarely the correct answer. Instead, she had to guess what the other person wanted her to say.

"Lovely," she answered.

"How are you settling in?"

She was saved by someone else stepping through the door. She recognised the old man who had threatened to expose her in the tailor's changing room.

"How may I help?" she asked him, but he ignored her and strode up to the antiques dealer.

"I hope you're not thinking of selling that Louis XVI chair to Littleton, Brown!" the old man rumbled, brandishing his walking stick.

"Lord Oldwell, good morning. No, I have no such plans. Why, may I ask? Are you interested in that chair?"

"Heavens, no! That monstrosity? I just don't want him to have it. He mentioned at the club that he wanted it. You make sure he doesn't get it, young man."

Rupert looked at least ten years older than Grazia, so he would have been a young man in the last century. At least his existence had been acknowledged, however, unlike her own.

"Yes, your Lordship," Rupert replied.

"Good day." The old man strutted out of the shop without a look at Grazia.

"Will you miss out on a sale just because he ordered you to do that?" Grazia asked Rupert.

He smiled mischievously. "I've already sold that chair."

"To Littleton?"

Rupert chuckled. "Even better—to that old man's wife!"

"Oh, dear. The poor lady is going to be in trouble. Her husband hates the chair."

"She'll be fine. Somebody said once that the man is head of the family but the woman is the neck that turns it. Lady Oldwell is a lot younger than her husband, so she can easily turn him wherever she wants."

He winked at Grazia, who felt her cheeks on fire. She had rarely been so happy to see her mother appear.

Rupert walked up to Rosaria.

"Good morning. I'm Rupert Brown, the antiques dealer next door. You must be Rosaria."

Rosaria smiled coquettishly. "I am she. Welcome to my shop."

She swept her arm as if showing a kingdom.

Rupert caught her hand mid-sweep and did a little bow as if he was about to kiss it, but didn't quite. Then the two of them chatted about Calcotbury, the virtues of country versus city living, and the latest meteorological events for all the time it took Grazia to completely unpack four boxes of bronze-die spaghetti.

Rupert straightened up, looking like he was about to leave.

Rosaria smiled. "Excuse the mess," she told him. "We are working hard to get everything ready for tomorrow. But you must visit us again once we are up and running."

"I certainly will."

CHAPTER 11

Once Rupert had disappeared into his shop with the Louis XVI chair in the window, Rosaria turned to Grazia. "Now, that's a charming man worth marrying!"

Grazia didn't find him so charming. There was something fox-like about the man's pointy face. Could her mother be right? After all, "Grazia Brown" or "Grace Brown" didn't sound too bad. An ordinary British surname.

It was nice of her mother to be thinking of potential matches for her. Sometimes Grazia felt that her mother wasn't keen on her ever finding a soulmate. Clearly she had been wrong.

Rosaria sighed. "He's just a little too young."

"Young?"

"For me." Rosaria patted her curls.

Grazia was instantly deflated. Her mother hadn't thought about her at all.

"Who are those youngsters waving at you from the window?" Rosaria asked.

Earlier that morning, Grazia had let herself into Rebecca's house. Rebecca had asked Grazia to keep an eye on the three boys while she was in Italy. Finding the teenagers asleep, she had left them a note. Her mother's question left her thinking that they had come to the shop to get food.

Grazia put down the box of amaretti and looked up. It wasn't the boys at the window. It was the tailor's daughters! It was sweet of them to wave to her, but why do it in front of Rosaria? Grazia smiled back at them gingerly.

"Who are they?" Rosaria asked.

"The daughters of the tailor."

At the mention of the man, her mother pursed her lips. "You wouldn't tell from those clothes they're wearing!"

"Ripped jeans are the fashion."

Grazia smiled apologetically at the girls, just in case they had lip-read Rosaria's words.

Thankfully, they saw the "Closed" sign on the door, waved again and left. Grazia let out a breath.

“How do they know you?”

“They were at the tailor’s shop when I went to collect the dress.”

She would stick to the truth as long as she could, but that wouldn’t be long if the girls decided to walk in and chat with her. She had been lucky this time, but what about tomorrow and the next day?

Once the deli was open, she’d be a sitting target. The tailor himself might come in to buy a leg of prosciutto for a change from his roast chicken. Heaven forbid, he might even come in to tell her that her dress was ready!

Doctors had patient confidentiality; priests had the secret of the confessional. Was there such a thing as a secret of the changing room for tailors?

This afternoon, as soon as her mother put her feet up, she must go to the tailor and instruct him to keep their dealings classified.

Rosaria narrowed her eyes. "What happened to the purple dress you wore at your British citizenship ceremony? I see it's missing from your wardrobe."

Grazia's heart leapt to her throat.

“It’s… at the dry cleaner’s.”

She’d have to talk to the town’s dry cleaner too.

CHAPTER 12

"If I man can't stand up for himself,

You're better off staying on the shelf."

—From The Sicilian Mama's "How to Pick a Husband" blog.

Grazia believed that there were times in life when a sandwich would suffice for lunch.

With the electrician due to come in the afternoon, a lot of sorting out still to do in the deli and those very important talks with the dry cleaner and the tailor, today was one of those days.

Rosaria, however, didn't agree with sandwich lunches on principle and had pulled a face when Grazia had suggested it. This was why Grazia was cutting up tomatoes for a pasta sauce for their lunch.

Rosaria walked in. "I've been to the market."

"Lunch is already underway. It's

too late to change it."

This wouldn't be the first time Rosaria tried to change the lunch plans after Grazia had already started preparations.

"I haven't bought food. I bought myself a T-shirt of Jesus. Look."

Grazia turned around to view, still chopping.

"That's Che Guevara."

"Who's that?"

"He was a Marxist revolutionary from Argentina."

"Never mind. He looks like Jesus." She put the T-shirt on and walked to the hall to admire herself in the mirror, then returned.

"On my way back I walked past the tea room. It's always the same people in there. They seem to spend their days doing nothing but sipping cups of tea and chatting while some of us work ourselves into the ground," Rosaria said, then sat down at the table and drained the glass of water that Grazia had put out at her place.

Meanwhile, Grazia stirred the chopped tomatoes into the sizzling pan.

"Some people are just lazy," Rosaria continued, helping herself to the bread Grazia had sliced and put in a basket on the table in front of her.

"Those who don't want to work shouldn't eat either, Saint Paul said," Rosaria added.

Grazia dressed the salad and put it on the table.

"I bet those people in the tea room are younger than me while I, at my age, am moving town, opening a deli and running a business."

She helped herself to another slice of bread while Grazia stirred the spaghetti with one hand and the sauce with the other.

"Some people just do not know what hard work means, I suppose.

Where is the oil?"

Grazia put the olive oil on the table and refilled the cheese mill before rushing back to the hob to stir the pots.

"Lunch is ready," she said, finally.

"Tomato sauce pasta again?" Rosaria asked, twisting her mouth.

Grazia opened her mouth to say that, with all the work required to open the deli, she had been too busy to shop for their meals. Then she stopped herself. Why should she justify herself?

Her mother had done barely any work. All she seemed to have

achieved that morning was buy a T-shirt printed with the face of a man she didn't know. So she smiled instead.

"If you would like something different, then next time you could stop at the greengrocer and buy some cauliflower, greens or whatever else you would like on your pasta."

Rosaria's eyes widened. "Mind how you speak to your mother, Disgrazia."

A shiver ran down Grazia's back. This was why she hated contradicting Rosaria. The woman had the power to make her feel small and wrong with a movement of her eyes, a flick of an eyebrow, a muttered word.

For the rest of the meal they ate in silence while Grazia's mind wandered.

What if Rosaria demanded to live with her after she married The One? What if he saw how Rosaria treated her and realised that she wasn't worthy of love?

He and Rosaria might even gang up against her, or Rosaria might take a dislike to him and treat him so badly that he'd run away.

Grazia chased the thoughts out of her mind.

CHAPTER 13

After the meal, Grazia washed up as quickly as she could while her mother went to her room, allegedly to read her magazines.

When Grazia had finished tidying up the kitchen, Rosaria was already snoring. Grazia grabbed a dress from her cupboard at random and hurried to the dry cleaner's.

"It's not in my interest to say this, but you can wash this dress in your washing machine," the dry cleaner told Grazia when she handed the dress over.

"I know, but I want you to have it," Grazia replied.

The man looked mystified but took it. The next stop was the tailor's.

Grazia lingered outside the door, steeling herself for the difficult conversation ahead. He was going to judge her, of course.

Over the years, anybody who had ever had a glimpse into her

relationship with her mother had judged her. Back when they were at school, Rebecca had often urged her to stand up to Rosaria. But if she hadn't done it back then, when she was a teenager and rebelling was expected of her, how could she do it now that she was fifty and should be kind to an elderly parent?

Of course the tailor was going to judge her. Grazia hated judgment even more than she hated asking for favours.

As she walked into the shop, the voice of Lord Oldwell hit her like a hurricane.

"And I found the very chair in my sitting room! My wife's doing, of course. Women are the bane of humanity! Adam would still be in the garden of Eden if it hadn't been for Eve!" the man pontificated from atop the same stool where Grazia had stood the day before. It was no Greek statue's plinth for him, but a soapbox, she decided.

The man seemed more accustomed to talking—make that shouting—than listening. Right now his view of womankind made Grazia dislike him so much that it was liberating. It meant that she didn't care anymore what he thought of her. So she strutted in boldly.

"Actually, I beg to differ."

The two men turned towards her, Lord Oldwell with the surprise of someone who isn't used to being contradicted. It was clear neither man had heard the door chime.

"Prisons hold more men than women," Grazia pointed out. "What's more, there have been way more wars, brutalities and genocides committed by men than by women."

"Your dress isn't ready," the tailor told her through a mouthful of pins he was holding between his lips. He didn't seem pleased by her interruption.

"I haven't come for a fitting," she told him. "I wanted to have a word."

"Yes?" he asked, still holding on to the pins.

"In private."

"Then I'm afraid you'll have to wait," he warned.

She checked her watch. The electrician was due at the deli in ten minutes. If the man found the shop shut, would he ring the bell of their flat and wake her mother from her siesta?

"I haven't got much time."

"Could you return later?"

No. The longer she left it, the higher the chances of Rosaria finding out about the dress. "I'll wait."

Hector Gonzales pulled a high stool over from his worktable and offered it to Grazia.

She could usually climb up on that kind of stool if she held onto the table and pulled herself up. Without a table, as she tried to mount it, she found herself stuck, with one half of her body on the stool and the other half dangling off.

She shouldn't have attempted the climb, she knew. Now it was too late to pretend that she preferred to stand up. She was stuck in the indecorous position in the middle of the room, all before the eyes of the two men.

The tailor stepped towards her and offered her an arm. She was in no position to decline it.

She contemplated whether she should use it to complete her climb or to return to the ground. However, as soon as she touched it, the tailor moved it higher, making this the arm equivalent of a leg-up. Now she was fully on the stool.

The tailor resumed working on the

hem of Lord Oldwell's trousers and Grazia tried to entertain herself by looking at her hands. Perched high on the stool, unable to get down on her own, she felt like a bird in a cage. She certainly wasn't about to burst into song.

"Too short!" Lord Oldwell boomed. For a moment, Grazia thought he was talking about her.

"Is this better?" the tailor asked after letting out a little more fabric.

"Longer!"

Lord Oldwell's vocabulary clearly didn't stretch as far as the word "please".

"With a break like this we would need cuffs," the tailor suggested.

"Then make the blasted cuffs, man!"

Grazia's blood boiled. She felt insulted by proxy. How dare the old grouch speak to this craftsman like that?

She was about to unleash her tongue on Lord Oldwell when he disappeared into the changing room.

Even from there Lord Oldwell could be heard muttering complaints and, on finally leaving the shop, he somehow managed to make even his goodbye sound impolite.

CHAPTER 14

"How can I help you?" the tailor asked her. His tone was weary.

"I would like to..."

She had prepared to ask him to keep their interactions confidential.

"...get off this stool," she said instead.

"Of course." He offered her his arm again.

She tried to put as little weight on it as she could while also holding her skirt so it didn't twist around her body as she got off the stool.

When she was finally safely on the ground, she gathered herself.

"You wanted to talk to me in private?" he prompted gently.

"I want you to keep our interactions confidential," she told him.

"Pardon?"

"Me coming to you to have my dress altered, you accepting the job, you doing the work and me coming for fittings. All these things must remain between us."

"Why?"

"My mother must not find out."

"Is the dress hers?"

"No, it's mine."

He waited for her to elaborate, but she wasn't going to offer any explanation. Every time she tried to explain her mother to other people, she found herself more baffled and confused than them.

"No problem. I won't tell your mother—even if she were to come into the shop and ask me," he promised.

"Also, please don't tell anyone else," Grazia added.

"Why?"

"In case she gets to hear about it indirectly."

He frowned. "May I ask what your mother's issue is with this dress?"

"No, you may not."

"As I'm working on the dress, I believe I ought to know."

It was a fair point. "She wants me to lose weight to fit into it. Alternatively, she would like to alter the dress herself."

"And you don't trust her to do the

job. I see."

Grazia felt he wasn't judging her—he really did understand her. Tension drained from her body and she felt a little taller.

The tailor sat on the stool where she had previously been. He was now almost at eye level with her. "This is why I got into tailoring. "

"Why?"

"I was a tall boy and my mother insisted on making my clothes. But I didn't want to wear those garments, with their elasticated waists and baggy legs. She wouldn't buy me anything from the shops, so I stole some of her sewing things and started altering the clothes she had made for me. At first, I didn't have a clue and I made them look even worse but, after a while, I managed to improve them."

Sympathy welled inside Grazia. "Your mother sounds a bit like mine. What happened when she discovered what you were doing? She must have worked it out when she washed and ironed your clothes."

"She was mad at me. She ordered me to give her back all the sewing stuff or I would get no pocket money ever again."

"What did you do?"

"I kept going, of course."

It had never been "of course" for Grazia. Openly disobeying her mother had always been too risky an option. Small, surreptitious acts of defiance were as far as she could ever go.

"I told her that I was going to become a tailor," Hector Gonzales went on. "I was only sixteen and had never considered tailoring as a career, but I had enjoyed making my own clothes, so I signed up for a tailoring apprenticeship. My mother didn't approve."

Was he judging Grazia for not standing up to her mother?

"Not everyone can rebel against their parents like that," she said defensively.

It was easy for him to preach. He had his own shop and income while she shared the deli with her mother. Rosaria's name was on the shop sign!

"It's easier to do it when your livelihood doesn't depend on them," Grazia said.

"I was sixteen. My livelihood did depend on my parents."

So he *was* judging her! She folded her arms over her chest.

"You might have been rebellious and independent when you were young, but you've lost some of that along the way!"

"What do you mean?" the tailor asked.

"The way you put up with Lord Oldwell's rudeness and bent over backwards for him."

"I didn't bend over backwards for Lord Oldwell. I sent him away when I was serving you the other day. Today he had an appointment and you didn't. I always respect my appointments," he finished stiffly.

"That doesn't mean that you

should stoop down and be servile."

"It's hard to work on the hem of someone's trousers without stooping," he pointed out.

"It was a metaphor!"

"Whatever that means."

"Yes, well, your lack of literary education doesn't justify Lord Oldwell being rude to you," Grazia insisted.

He widened his eyes. "I don't lack literary education, actually. What's more, you might find that the one being rude to me is not Lord Oldwell!"

The door chimes sounded like the

bell of a boxing ring. Their match was over and another customer was stepping into the shop.

Grazia wanted to remind the tailor to keep quiet about her visits and her dress, but this wasn't a good time to request anything from him.

He was already greeting the new customer, so Grazia gave a terse goodbye and left.

The electrician was waiting at the door of the deli. He must have rung the bell of their flat without managing to wake up Rosaria.

He plugged and unplugged the display counter fridges, and his surprise in seeing that they still didn't work told Grazia how little faith he had had in her diagnosis.

He pulled the fridges apart, went back and forth to the van to get tools and pieces, then back to the offices to get more pieces. Unfortunately the fridges couldn't be repaired without a spare part that he didn't have with him.

"I'll come back as soon as we've got the part," he said nonchalantly, climbing into his van.

"Wait! We have to open the deli tomorrow."

He shrugged.

"Aren't you going to give us a courtesy fridge?"

"Sorry?"

"Car repair shops lend courtesy cars."

He snorted. "We don't do 'courtesy fridges'. We'll give you a ring when the piece is in stock and we can arrange another visit."

She watched him drive away with a sinking heart. How was she going to tell Rosaria that they couldn't open tomorrow?

One good thing could be that Rebecca might be back in time for their opening. This made Grazia

decided that, at some point today, she must go and check on Rebecca's sons.

CHAPTER 15

"Steer clear of the crazy, the cheater, the crafty, the cad.

Watch out for the loafer, the loser, the lenient dad."

—From The Sicilian Mama's "How to Pick a Husband" blog.

Rosaria didn't take the postponement of the deli's

opening well.

"It's a conspiracy against foreigners!" she accused, finger in the air.

"No, it's not. The fridges were broken."

"They've been sabotaged, then!"

Grazia sighed. "They came sealed from the factory. The factory workers couldn't know whether they were for an Italian deli or a local butcher."

"We'll never be accepted in this town," Rosaria insisted, letting herself sink down onto the sofa.

"That's not true. We haven't had any trouble here and we've been welcomed warmly."

"It's all been a pretence. They'll strike as soon as we lower our guard. Don't trust anyone: it's just you and me against the world," Rosaria snapped.

Since the arson attack on their former restaurant, back in London, Rosaria had doubled down on her theory of it being "them against the world." Finding the restaurant on fire had shaken her so much that she hadn't objected when Rebecca had suggested they both leave the city and move to her small, friendly village.

In Calcotbury, Rebecca had assured them, people were nice and welcoming. An Italian deli would go down a treat on the main street. Rebecca ought to know, because her antiques shop was on the main street and was doing very well.

"What are we going to do with the fresh ricotta and the mozzarellas?" Rosaria asked now in a tone of challenge, as if Grazia had orchestrated the delay for some nefarious purpose of her own.

"We could give them away for free," Grazia suggested.

"Give stuff away for free?"

The concept was clearly one Rosaria couldn't comprehend.

"Yes. For publicity."

"You must be out of your mind!" her mother scoffed.

"We could use them in a pre-opening party. It would help us get to know the town and the town to know us."

Rosaria scowled. "You know I hate parties."

They couldn't reach an agreement so Grazia got on with rearranging the shop in view of the delayed opening.

When Rosaria began enquiring about what was going to be

for supper—which usually was the sign that she was hungry—Grazia understood that it was time she started cooking.

"I'll sacrifice myself and eat some of the mozzarella if you make pizza to go with it," Rosaria announced magnanimously.

On such a busy day as this, making pizza dough wouldn't have been Grazia's first choice, but it was true that the mozzarella needed using up.

She went upstairs and commenced kneading.

At suppertime Rosaria ate the mozzarella, even without the pizza, with such gusto that Grazia started to believe in a different conspiracy theory about the fridges' breakdown: perhaps her mother had sabotaged them so that she could binge guilt-free on expensive mozzarella.

By the time Grazia was able to leave the flat to go and check on Rebecca's boys it was almost eight o'clock.

They would be getting ready for bed, Grazia thought. All three were in their teens so all she would have to do, surely, was ask if they'd brushed their teeth, wish them goodnight and leave. She could manage that.

Rebecca didn't live above her shop like Grazia or the tailor. Rebecca's Antiques occupied three floors of the high street's sixteenth-century building, while she and her sons lived in a stylishly converted barn on the edge of Calcotbury.

The barn conversion had been a triumph. Rebecca's was the most beautiful house Grazia had ever seen in real life. It was definitely no longer suitable for cattle!

Her friend and her children had moved to Calcotbury from London after Rebecca's divorce some nine years ago. Grazia and Rebecca had drifted apart during the years of Rebecca's marriage, due to a combination of embarrassed reticence (Rebecca's) and misplaced envy (Grazia's).

Their friendship had been reignited quickly when Grazia had moved to Calcotbury, but the missed years of seeing the boys grow up had left a permanent impact on Grazia's relationship with them. They felt to her like strangers.

This made it very awkward for her to be in charge of them during their mother's unexpected absence.

It didn't help that they were boys

and not girls, either. Boys, like men, were exotic and mysterious creatures from a distant kingdom. "Keep away from boys," had been the extent of her own sex education. "Don't act like a boy," her social etiquette training. "Don't let boys break your heart," her emotional advice.

Boys were the forbidden fruit that her body and heart longed for, but which, if reached out for and plucked, would get you ejected from paradise.

As a result, all through her youth she had kept away from them, and now she had no idea how they worked.

CHAPTER 16

Rebecca had told her that the boys would feed themselves and more or less clean up after themselves, but it would be nice if she could "check on them." Grazia had no idea what she was supposed to check for.

To Rebecca it must have seemed

like a reasonable request. She surely had had no idea that, for her friend, it was like being asked to climb Mount Everest with a blindfold. What was she supposed to check? Whether their school shirts were ironed? If they had killed each other?

Music wafted out of the house as she approached. It didn't sound like a lullaby. Or was it a teenagers' version of one?

The music drowned the sound of the doorbell. She pressed it again and rapped on the door with her knuckles.

Nobody came.

She remembered that Rebecca had given her a key in case the boys locked themselves out. She found it in her bag and tried to unlock the door, only to find that it was already unlocked.

Maybe this was what she was here for—to remind the boys of things like needing to lock the door at night.

She stepped into the entrance hall. The noise increased.

"Hello?" she called.

Nobody heard her.

A girl walked out of the study, saw her and did a double take.

"Oh, hi," she said, looking as

surprised as Grazia.

What was a girl doing in Rebecca's house? Rebecca hadn't mentioned anything about girls visiting, nor whether that was allowed or not.

Why did this girl look familiar? For an absurd moment Grazia asked herself if Rebecca had ever mentioned having a daughter.

Definitely not. Maybe she was her fiancé's daughter. A girl cousin.

The girl spoke again. "Your dress is coming along nicely. Dad was working on it when we left home."

This was why she was familiar. She was the tailor's youngest daughter!

Even with this new knowledge things still didn't make any sense.

"What are you doing here?"

"We came to the party," she answered.

A party! Did Rebecca know about this? A shiver ran down Grazia's back. Wouldn't Rebecca have warned her if she had known a party was planned?

She must tell her friend. Or must she?

Rebecca had enough problems on her plate, what with being stuck in a foreign country during an international paralysis of air travel. No, she couldn't burden her friend with it. She would have to deal with this one on her own.

She strode past the girl and into the living room. As she opened the door the music hit her like a wall.

She hadn't known what to expect. She hadn't been to any parties when she was young and, these days, the only parties she attended were other people's weddings.

For a moment she couldn't register the details of the scene. All she saw was darkness, fog and shapes moving about.

She reminded herself that, at eighteen, George was legally an adult. Technically there was an adult in charge of this party.

At one end of Rebecca's cream sofa someone was eating a floppy pizza straight from its cartoon. At the other end someone else was drinking what looked like red wine. Had the boys considered covering Rebecca's beloved sofa with a splashproof rug?

People were smoking. What about the ash? Rebecca didn't own a single ashtray, Grazia knew.

The curtains and the upholsteries were going to be impregnated with the smell of smoke for ever! She had to stop this party!

"George!" she shouted.

Nobody came forward. Grazia tapped a dancing boy on the shoulder.

"Where is George?"

The boy pointed the neck of his beer bottle towards the stairs, sloshing liquid on Rebecca's eggshell-blue carpet. Grazia immediately dabbed at it with a cloth she found lying on the floor, only to realise that the "cloth" was a girl's white cardigan.

She dropped it back on the floor with guilt and irritation. This party had to stop before more damage could be done.

"Where is George?" she asked a girl who was swaying to the music at the foot of the stairs.

"He's with Ella. In his bedroom."

Grazia reeled, then steadied herself on the banisters. Girls and boys in bedrooms? She started up the stairs, then stopped. Was she really going to burst into George's bedroom upstairs? She must ask another parent for help.

She'd often regretted missing out on motherhood, but right now she was glad not to have been blessed with children to raise.

Humans should be born fully adult and self-sufficient, she decided. If that wasn't possible, they should be entrusted to well-trained, vetted parents. The current system was absurd. Here she was—unvetted and definitely untrained—in charge not only of Rebecca's children and her immaculate house, but also of a bunch of other people's kids.

She didn't know the parents of any of the other kids except for one. The tailor!

They hadn't parted on the best of terms, but Hector Gonzales was Grazia's only option. She all but ran

out of Rebecca's house and back to the main street.

CHAPTER 17

The shop was shut at this time, of course. Grazia rang the bell of the flat and thumped the door with her fists. "Help!"

Heavy footsteps pounded downstairs and the door opened.

"Hello," Hector said cautiously.

"I have bad news. One of your

daughters is at a party with boys!"

"I hope not it's not just one of my daughters. The three of them were supposed to stay together," he replied.

"I saw your youngest, anyway."

Was Ella the name of his eldest? If so, would it reassure him to know that she was at the party too, but in George's bedroom?

"Your other daughters might be there. I don't know."

"Where is 'there'?"

"The house of my friend, Rebecca. She asked me to check on her sons while she's away. When I got there, I found pandemonium!"

"What sort of pandemonium?"

"Loud music, dancing... But more might be going on upstairs and they're wrecking my friend's house!"

"Well, we can't have that. I'll grab the car keys. Meet me at the car round the back."

He closed the door and disappeared upstairs, leaving Grazia to wonder about his priorities.

He was already sitting in his small car with the engine running when Grazia found her way to the back of the building. He set off even before she'd done up her seatbelt.

"Should we call the police?" Grazia fretted.

"Is anyone injured?"

"I don't think so, but it's still an unauthorised party."

He studied her for a moment, still driving. "Have you ever done anything naughty in your life?" he asked in a tone of pure, non-judgemental curiosity.

"Plenty, if you ask my mother."

"I'm asking you."

She squirmed in her seat. The naughty things other people did were rebellious and "cool". Hers were not.

They were petty little acts of

revenge, like removing the batteries from the TV remote control so that Rosaria couldn't switch channels when Grazia's favourite show was about to start. Like taking her dress to the tailor against her mother's wishes. Or hiding a box of chocolates under her bed so that she could eat them secretly without being teased by Rosaria.

The tailor stopped the car before they reached the house. The air around them vibrated with music. Hector unfolded himself out of the car and strode up the path with Grazia catching up behind him.

"The entrance is that way," she told him.

"We're not going through the front door."

"If you're intending to surprise them, I can tell you we could walk straight into the living room and nobody would notice!"

He continued walking towards the kitchen entrance and she followed.

On her earlier survey of the party, Grazia hadn't visited the kitchen. If she had, she would have gone to fetch help immediately.

Rebecca's designer kitchen was scattered with empty takeaway boxes, melting tubs of ice cream, bottles and drink cans. Grazia had never seen so much as an orange peel on these pristine counters. The boys would have to work hard to return the house to its original state. Would they be able to do it before their mother's return? Grazia would have to help them, no doubt.

As they stepped into the living room, the scene before them was even worse than what Grazia had witnessed earlier. Young people were dancing on the dining table, chairs and coffee table. Plant pots had been overturned. One girl was dancing on the piano stool, jumping up and down with the music. Occasionally she slipped and one foot tramped on the piano keyboard.

The house that Rebecca had built and furnished to perfection was being ruined. Did the tailor plan just to take his daughters away, or would he help Grazia deal with the rest of the party?

Her own father, she knew, would have ripped through the room like a hurricane in search of his daughter. There would have been shouts, tears and threats of cataclysmic punishments.

But nothing like that happened. Instead, the tailor quietly walked over to the sound system and turned it off. He then switched on all the ceiling lights. Most of the kids stopped dancing immediately, while a few continued for a few more seconds, then opened their eyes and stopped.

"Hey! Who turned the music off?" someone protested.

No one replied. Complete silence fell on the room as everyone saw the tailor, who was standing in the middle of the room like a silent mountain.

"Party's over. Time to tidy up," he said calmly.

"Yes, Mr Gonzales," the kids responded.

They all seemed to know him. Probably it was through his daughters. And clearly they respected him.

"Hello, Dad." His two youngest daughters came forward with guilty looks.

"When you told me that you were going to a party at here, you didn't tell me that Mrs Lewis was away," he said, scowling.

They looked at their feet. "Sorry."

"Where is Ella?" he asked.

"Probably upstairs with George."

Oh, no! Grazia could imagine the scene: the father bursts through the door, finds daughter and boyfriend kissing, and then kills everyone!

No, this wasn't Sicily back in the old days. Grazia still wanted to save the girl from the indignity and punishment that was sure to follow, though. She ran up the stairs, knocked on George's bedroom door and whispered urgently. "Ella's father is here!"

The door opened and George and Ella appeared, both fully clothed.

Inside the room, Grazia saw a chessboard on the floor with a game underway.

"Hi, Grazia. Is everything alright?" George asked with surprise.

"Ella's father is coming upstairs. Don't worry; he doesn't look mad and he's not armed!"

"Oh, no, Dad's going to be cross with me for leaving my sisters downstairs unsupervised," Ella said with a groan. "I hate being the eldest. It's not fair!"

"We don't like loud music so we came up to play chess in peace," George explained.

Ella left George and Grazia and stomped down the stairs, muttering to herself that she wasn't her sisters' mother. It looked as though she would be the one doing the scolding.

"Are you feeling all right, Grazia?" George asked, catching the expression on her face.

"This place! Your mother is going to have a fit."

"Don't worry. We'll tidy up before Mum gets home."

"There's more than tidying up to do—there's repairs and mending. I don't know how you'll get red wine stains off your mum's cream sofa."

"What? I bet it was one of Luke's friends! I told him not to invite them," George growled.

Grazia watched him storm downstairs to tell his brother off. If she could learn from these two how to flip one's position from guilty to righteous instantly, she would enjoy life a lot more.

The door of Rebecca's bedroom opened and a girl stepped out. She was wearing Rebecca's wedding dress!

"I'm getting married," she announced.

CHAPTER 18

"A good husband is steady and calm.

In every crisis his presence is a balm."

—From The Sicilian Mama's "How to Pick a Husband" blog.

Grazia was almost paralysed with shock. Only a chosen few

—mother, sister, best friend—were allowed to see a woman's wedding dress before the day. Someone actually wearing it was on another level of horror.

"This is George's mum's wedding dress," she managed to say in a chocked voice.

"I found it, so it's mine now," the girl said, pouting.

Her eyes were unfocused.

"No, it's not. Take it off," Grazia demanded, stepping towards her.

"It's mine!" the girl protested and took a step backward.

There was a horrible ripping

sound.

"You've torn it! Take it off at once!" Grazia lunged for the girl.

"I haven't!" The girl staggered, tripped on a discarded cola bottle and fell on the floor. "You made me fall!" she whined, trying to stand up but unable to coordinate her arms and legs, which were getting tangled in the dress's train. The bottle of cola, now on its side, was spilling brown liquid onto the dress and the cream carpet.

"Stop! Stop!" Grazia begged.

"What's happening?" It was the tailor's voice.

Relief flooded her.

"It's Rebecca's wedding dress!" she cried.

He reached the flailing girl and picked her up gently in his arms. She looked at him, doe-eyed and blissful. "You are my groom, Mr Gonzales."

They did look like bride and groom as Hector carried her, white train trailing behind him, back to the room where she'd come from. He put her down on a chair.

"When I close the door you will take off the dress and put your clothes back on because I need to repair this dress," he ordered.

She nodded, suddenly obedient. "Yes, because you are a tailor. Mum says you are a good tailor. She also says you were a very good husband. I want a good husband. Will I find one too?" the girl asked.

"I'm sure you will."

He left the room and closed the door.

"Now we have to hope she will do as I asked," he said to Grazia.

"You certainly have a way with..."

"Inebriated people?"

"Actually I was going to say girls."

"I have three daughters."

"Not all fathers of daughters have

a gift like yours."

"You're paying me a compliment. Tonight is full of surprises," the tailor replied.

She felt her cheeks flush. Time to change the topic. "What will we do about the dress?" she asked, then regretted saying "we". "Sorry, I didn't mean that it's your responsibility. It wasn't your daughters who damaged it."

"Still, Rebecca is a friend," the tailor replied. "Tomorrow morning I'll take the dress and go to my fabric suppliers. As soon as I've got matching fabric, I'll start the repair. Timing is going to be tight, unfortunately, and I haven't even finished your dress yet."

"Forget about my dress. And I'm paying for the fabric," she said.

"Why should you?"

"I was left in charge of the boys. If I had come earlier, the party wouldn't have happened."

"Then we'll go half."

"All right," Grazia agreed. "And I'm coming to the fabric shop with you."

The words were out of her mouth before she had thought about them.

"Okay. I'll pick you up from your home in the morning."

"No!" she cried with alarm.

If he picked her up from her home, Rosaria would notice. Arranging to be away for the morning would already be difficult enough without a man turning up to pick her up. "I mean, there's no need: I can walk to you. Give me a time and I'll be there."

"As you wish."

Together with Hector's girls and Rebecca's boys they tidied, cleared, cleaned and fixed as much as they could that night.

When it was time to go home, Hector turned to her. "I'll give you a lift home."

No way! Rosaria would be waiting at the window.

"I'm happy to walk."

"Not at this hour. Where do you live?"

"You can drop me off at the beginning of the high street, then."

He didn't insist, even though Grazia could tell that it pained him to leave her at a crossroads in the middle of the night.

It turned out to have been a wise decision, because Rosaria was waiting at the window. As soon as Grazia was upstairs, the questions started.

"What have you been doing until

this hour?" Rosaria asked, fists planted on hips and hair curlers sticking out like horns.

"I had to check on Rebecca's boys."

"What took so long?"

"They needed help."

Years of experience had taught Grazia that Rosaria used information as ammunition, so it was always better to give her the least possible.

"What for?"

"Clearing up their supper." It wasn't far from the truth.

Rosaria must have been tired because she didn't ask anything more and let her retreat to her bedroom.

The events of the day swirled in Grazia's mind. The tailor turning off the music and making the party stop, taming the girl in the wedding dress, driving the car home with his daughters in the back and Grazia in the front, close enough to touch him.

With him next to her she had felt safe. Together they were going to fix Rebecca's house and her wedding dress. It was all going to be okay.

CHAPTER 19

"I've got to run an errand for Rebecca. I'll be gone all morning," Grazia announced to Rosaria at breakfast.

Her mother frowned. "What would you have done if we were opening the deli today?"

"I've agreed to run this errand only

because we're not."

"What errand is it?"

"Something to do with her wedding dress."

"I love wedding dresses. I'll come with you," Rosaria said, beginning to smile.

"You can't. Nobody can see her wedding dress before the day."

"You are," her mother protested.

"I'm her best friend."

"Are you?" Rosaria smirked. "Then why didn't she make you her bridesmaid?"

She always knew how to strike Grazia where it hurt.

"You know very well why."

"The fact that her fiancé's daughters have to be bridesmaids doesn't mean that you couldn't be one, too."

Not true. Grazia couldn't be a bridesmaid. Charles' daughters were pretty young things while she was old enough to be their mother. Together they would have made a terrible assortment. She wasn't going to give Rosaria the satisfaction of admitting that.

"I didn't want to be one."

"Really?" Rosaria asked with a mocking smile. "And where are you going this morning for your 'best friend'?"

"Bristol."

Stick to the truth as much as possible, Grazia reminded herself.

"How will you get there?"

Grazia felt her armpits go clammy. Rosaria's interrogations always left her like this.

"A friend of Rebecca is driving."

"She has a car, then?"

Rosaria was assuming that Rebecca's friend was a woman. Grazia wasn't going to correct her.

"Yes."

"Rebecca should sort out her

own wedding-dress issues instead of inconveniencing all her friends."

"She's still in Italy."

"All the same."

Rosaria liked to have the last word so Grazia didn't respond. She just prayed that the interrogation could be over.

"Off you go, but come back for lunch, of course," Rosaria said.

It was all Grazia could do not to whoop with happiness. She had manged to wangle the whole morning off!

The tailor was already in the car when Grazia met him at the back of his shop at eight on the dot. Hector looked happy to see her, but the dark shadows under his eyes told her that he might not have had a restful night. But of course he wouldn't have: he was a single parent.

"I'm on time," she announced as if to reassure herself that his tiredness couldn't be her fault.

"I didn't say you weren't."

He smiled, and for the first time she noticed a cheeky dimple on one cheek. She had to tear her gaze away to stop herself staring.

"I'm ready to go."

The sooner they set off, the sooner

she could stop thinking about the man and start concentrating on the task at hand.

Just like the night before, he started driving when she was still battling with her seatbelt.

"Isn't driving a bit like using a sewing machine?" she asked when they were out of the town.

"What makes you say that?" he asked, keeping his eyes on the road.

"Both have pedals, lines to follow, the ability to reverse and...a certain element of danger."

He laughed. "I've never seen things that way."

She had never heard him laugh and it surprised her how that sound seemed to reach right inside and fill her chest with lightness.

They stopped at a T-junction.

"I think you ought to pay attention here. There are cars coming from both directions."

He smiled. "I can see that."

He looked both ways, waited, then looked again before turning right onto a bigger road. The car picked up speed.

"What's the speed limit here?" Grazia asked.

"Sixty."

"You're doing sixty-one!"

"Speedometers underread."

"I see." But she didn't.

"Are you always a nervous passenger or is it just with me?" Hector asked her.

"I'm not a nervous passenger," she protested.

Actually, she had no idea whether she was or not. The truth was that she hadn't been in a car for a long time. Neither she or Rosaria had a driving licence or a car, and travelling by taxi was expensive. Her only method of transport was buses, in which she never sat at the front. It meant that she wasn't used to seeing the road whizz past so fast. It scared her a bit.

They drove in silence for a little while, then he spoke casually. "Do you know what happens when you pull the handbrake on a car that's moving at sixty miles per hour?"

"No idea."

"The rear wheels lock and the car spins one hundred and eighty degrees, like in the car chases of action movies."

"Why are you telling me?" Heaven forbid he wanted to demonstrate!

"Because you keep putting your hand on my handbrake," he

explained.

"Sorry." Grazia snatched her hand back. "I'm scared. I don't travel by car often."

Hector slowed down immediately.

CHAPTER 20

The fabric wholesaler was in a dome-shaped warehouse, much like an aeroplane hangar. Grazia imagined aeroplanes with canvas wings flying out of the hangar, then sailing boats with waxed sails. Clothes and curtains, draping and upholstery—a world of fabric rolling out of the great hangar doors.

In the anteroom the attendant greeted them with a smile. He seemed to know the tailor and welcomed him with questions about how he was.

Hector laid Rebecca's dress onto the worktop. "I need just enough fabric to replace this panel," he said, showing the man what was needed.

"I didn't know you made wedding dresses," the man said.

"This is a personal project."

A broad smile spread across the man's face. "Congratulations, Hector! Many, many congratulations!" He took the tailor's hand and shook it.

Did he think that the tailor was getting married, Grazia wondered. Suddenly it dawned on her that that wasn't such a preposterous idea. The tailor wasn't too old. After all, was one ever too old for marriage?

He wasn't bad-looking either, and he seemed to be a thoroughly nice man. The image of him carrying the girl in the wedding dress the night before flashed across Grazia's mind. He had looked strong and protective, nothing short of a good husband.

The attendant's congratulatory smile shifted to Grazia.

"Congratulations to you, too," he told her.

She was puzzled. What did he mean?

"Oh, no, it's not us who are getting married," the tailor said.

It finally dawned on Grazia that the man had assumed that the tailor was marrying her. Instant heat bloomed on her cheeks and she burst into a nervous chuckle.

"Definitely not me—if you look at the size of the dress, for a start!"

An awkward silence followed. There was no safe way for a man to react to a woman's comment about her body. Agreeing might offend her self-image, but disagreeing might offend her intelligence. Grazia felt sorry for putting the man in this situation and came to the rescue. “Do you have any silk taffeta in this shade of white?”

The man smiled gratefully and held the gossamer-thin cloth between his thumb and forefinger. “I fear we might not have much left. Let’s see what we’ve got.”

Grazia had never seen so many rolls of fabric in one place. Countless shades of white, types of weave, accessories and embellishment all created a dazzling array. Ivory and champagne, taffetas and tulles, embroidered and sequinned, polyester and silk. Miles and miles of bridal possibilities. There must be enough there for her to be a bride one day, surely.

The three of them discussed the most appropriate fabric for the panel substitution. Grazia paid half the invoice, which was very reasonable.

After saying goodbye to the attendant, she and Hector loaded the dress and the fabric onto the back seat of the car and took their seats. This time, she noticed, he waited for her to buckle up before starting the engine.

"This fabric looks perfect. If anything gives us away to Rebecca now it will only be the craftmanship," she decided.

Telling Rebecca about the party was arguable, but there was no way she should know about the violation of her dress.

"You don't have much faith in me, do you?" Hector asked with a hint of sadness.

"I do! I wouldn't have given you my dress otherwise. But you've never done a wedding dress so there's no room for complacency, that's all."

"I never thought so. Certainly no room for complacency with you." He smiled and glanced at her.

"What's that supposed to mean?" she asked.

"That you are a demanding woman. It's not necessarily a criticism."

Grazia tried to focus on him saying "not necessarily", but it was the word "criticism" that lingered in her brain.

"Where do you live?" he asked as they took the turning for Calcotbury.

"That's quite a forward question."

"I'm only asking so that I can drop

you off at home."

"No need. I can walk."

Rosaria would be waiting at the window, watching for her.

"Calcotbury is a small town. How come I haven't seen you around before? Have you recently moved here?" he asked.

"I would rather not discuss personal matters."

That came out more chastising than she had meant and she was sorry about it.

"As you wish. It's just that, as you're a good friend of Rebecca's and in charge of her sons—among whom is my daughter's boyfriend—I had thought that we were more than customer and tailor."

She nodded. "When you put it that way... Yes, my mother and I have just moved to Calcotbury. It was Rebecca's suggestion."

"Where were you before?"

"Not in Calcotbury."

She didn't want to talk about the move because he was bound to ask why they left. Violence should bring shame on the violent, not the victim, yet it felt like a stain on herself that someone had hated her and Rosaria so much that they had set fire to their restaurant.

Thankfully the tailor was considerate enough not to ask any more.

CHAPTER 21

When they got to the shop, the answering machine's light was flashing reproachfully. Hector played back the messages and they revealed a torrent of needs.

Someone needed their trousers to be ready because they had a job interview. Someone else needed a jacket for a funeral. Another had only one pair of trousers left that fit him. The town's only tailor was in demand.

He sighed and ran a hand over his brow. Grazia felt the urge to hug him but kept her arms tight at her sides.

"I'll help you," she offered instead.

He raised his eyebrows.

"You do the difficult bits and I'll do the easier ones, as if I were your assistant," she added.

"I don't know what to say."

"You haven't much choice unless you'd rather leave the wedding dress entirely to me—which I don't recommend."

He was polite enough not to guffaw at the suggestion. "Well, thank you, then."

She cleared a chair for herself and he showed her the sewing machines, the drawers with the cotton reels, the most urgent jobs. She started with an easy hem for a pair of trousers that he had already basted.

"Have you any thimbles my size?" she asked, having tried a few that felt like eggcups over her fingers.

He walked to the counter where the till was and opened a little drawer tucked away in a corner. Grazia saw him hesitate, then he pulled something out and returned to her.

"You can use this."

It was a silver thimble.

"It's beautiful," she said, putting it on. It fit her perfectly. "But it's not your size."

"It was my wife's," he said quietly.

"I'm sorry. You don't have to let me use it."

She slipped it off her finger but he stopped her with his hand. It was warm and soft like a blanket.

"You can use it. My wife wasn't a seamstress, but she often volunteered to help me when I was overwhelmed with work. Just like you have offered to do," he said without looking at her.

"Thank you."

Grazia slipped her finger back into the thimble reverently. He hadn't given it to her. He had loaned it, she reminded herself.

They sat in companionable silence, he measuring and cutting the fabric for Rebecca's wedding dress at one end of the worktable, she at the other end, hemming the trousers of the man who had an interview tomorrow with tiny stitches.

She had never sewn for anyone other than family or friends so she felt all the responsibility of her job. If the hem were to come undone during the interview, the man would feel ill at ease and might not make a good impression on his prospective employer.

She kept her eyes on her work with laser focus. Even so, she was aware of her companion—where he was, what he was doing and what he was looking at.

Right now he was looking at her. She could feel it without glancing up. He wasn't looking at the thimble—if she was using it properly or damaging it. Nor was he looking at the hem she was stitching with near-invisible stitches. He was looking at her.

Rosaria never looked at her other than to scowl and intimidate. Rebecca was too busy to look at her even when they talked.

When she was younger, men had looked at her with desire, with flirtation, with indifference and even with scorn. No one had ever looked at her in a way that said, "I want to know you."

She must not look up and meet the tailor's gaze. She must not let him see that she was aware. It was certain to break the spell.

Because a spell it must be: there was no other explanation.

Her phone rang and it broke her concentration. She looked up and caught Hector, with the tailor's chalk in one hand and the scissors in the other, looking at her as if she were an infinitely mysterious creature of wonderment.

He snapped his gaze away and Grazia reached down into her bag to retrieve her phone. It was her mother.

"Hi."

"Disgrazia! Where are you? Where is my lunch?"

Oh, no, she had completely forgotten about lunch!

"I'm on my way."

"Where are you?"

"Almost home."

True. Exactly two roads away.

"I cannot hear any car noises."

"It's an electric car." Grazia shuddered. When she had to start lying it meant that she was cornered.

"You had better be here in the next ten minutes or you'll find a mother who has starved to death."

"I will. Bye."

Grazia ended the call before she had to say more lies. She felt her cheeks redden. There was no way the tailor hadn't heard her fib about the electric car. Possibly also her mother's side of the dialogue, too.

If he observed the way her mother treated her, he might start viewing Grazia through her mother's eyes and end up thinking less of her.

She looked up and met his gaze. There was no judgement there, she saw, just interest.

"What's Disgrazia?" he asked. "A pet name?"

"Not exactly. My name is Grazia."

"Grazia," he repeated.

"You say my name perfectly! That's

rare," she told him.

"My ancestors are Spanish and I know a bit of the language. It isn't so different from Italian. Is this why you told me that your name was Grace—because you thought I couldn't pronounce it?"

"Yes. Also because I didn't want my mother to find out about the dress. Besides, I wish I was called Grace."

"Grazia is much more beautiful."

He was doing it again. Hearing her name from his lips, in his voice, pronounced so well like he really knew her, made her dizzy. Nobody had ever spoken her name so beautifully. He spoke it like a piece of chocolate melting in the mouth.

"If you've got to go home to your mother, just go. Don't worry about me. Come back when you can—or don't, if you can't or don't want to," Hector told her.

God knew how much she wanted to! Even if only to have him look at her like he had done a few minutes ago, and say her name again.

"Thank you, Hector. May I call you that?"

"Of course, Grazia."

She almost skipped home, and not just because she needed to get there quickly. She felt like her feet were skimming the top of a cloud.

But clouds can bring storms.

CHAPTER 22

"That was a long trip," Rosaria greeted her.

"There was a lot of fabric to choose from." Grazia put on her kitchen apron.

"Why? It's not like you need to choose the colour with a wedding dress!"

Grazia bit her tongue and turned on the fire under the pasta water. Feeding others should be an act of love, but she had started to view food as a way to stopper Rosaria's mouth.

"I've changed my mind about the opening party. We should have one," Rosaria said.

Now? No, no, no! She had no time for that. She needed to help Hector with the wedding dress and his work, help erase the last traces of the party from Rebecca's house and keep a much closer eye on the boys.

"It's a bit late to organise an opening party now. It'll clash with the wedding."

"It won't be too late if you start thinking about my deli instead of your friend's silly wedding dress," Rosaria snapped.

This was attention-seeking and a threat. Her mother would insist on having an opening party, something she had never wanted, if Grazia continued disappearing.

"I will concentrate on the deli."

"So tomorrow you'll stay at the deli?"

This was tricky. How could she leave Hector to battle alone with the wedding dress and the flood of jobs that had poured into his shop?

"Tomorrow I can't."

"Why?" Rosaria peered at her with narrowed eyes.

When she looked at her like that, Grazia imagined her mother could see right inside her brain with all the secrets it held, including those Grazia kept from herself.

Like the fact that, even if she hadn't promised Hector that she would be back tomorrow, she was going to anyway. Not just because she felt she owed it to Rebecca, whose wedding dress had been ruined under Grazia's watch, but also because she had enjoyed it.

It was time to lie.

"Tomorrow I have to visit one of our suppliers."

"Who?"

The problem with lying was that she needed to think on her feet, remember her answers and be on guard all the time so that she wouldn't contradict herself.

"The fabric suppliers."

"What fabric?"

"I want to make jam tops and the breadbasket liners with the same fabric we have for our window curtains."

This was actually a lovely idea. The red and white gingham would look lovely splashed across the shop in little details.

"In fact, for a small extra charge, we could pack the customers' shopping into fabric bags instead of paper ones."

"You have never discussed this with me."

Suspicion was turning into offence.

"I want to see what price the supplier can do for us."

"Then I should come. You can't haggle."

This was another problem with

lies: they had a habit of slipping out of your control.

"It's far away. We'll need to take several buses and…" she tried to think what could put Rosaria off "… we won't be back until dinnertime."

Would the threat of missing her afternoon siesta put Rosaria off? Grazia crossed her fingers.

"You'd better cook me some lunch before you go, then," Rosaria said.

Grazia let out a tiny sigh of relief. "Of course."

With one bold fib she had earned herself an entire day off. She was going to spend it working with

Hector in his shop.

CHAPTER 23

"The path of physical attraction

Has led to many a war, death and destruction."

—From the Sicilian Mama's "How to Pick a Husband" blog.

"Hector?"

Grazia scanned the shop through the mannequins, past

the ironing board, along the shelves of fabric rolls.

She checked behind the till, the wattle-and-daub partition wall, by the changing cubicles. The shop's sign read "Open" and the door was unlocked, but Hector wasn't anywhere to be found.

The door to the stairs that led to his flat was ajar.

"Hector?" she called through the gap.

She would have stepped through the door and called upstairs if, the night before, she hadn't had an unsettling dream.

She had dreamt that she and Hector were strolling through a tunnel of roses in a beautiful English garden. When they got to the end of the tunnel, they stopped. He went down on one knee and asked her to marry him. She said yes and he put his late wife's thimble on her ring finger. The proposal was followed by a quick wedding. Then he was hauling her up these very stairs to his bedroom, which was like a caveman's lair, with animal skins draped on the floor and bed and a roaring fire.

The dream had rocked her not so much because of its plot—marriage to Hector—but because how happy she had felt in it. How disappointed she had been on waking up and discovering it had only been a dream.

This was absurd: she was waiting for The One. She had waited for him for fifty years. All through this time, while The One was getting lost and missing all the chances of meeting her that the Powers Above had put on his path, she had remained faithful. Was Grazia going to let lust lead her astray to another man?

Just then, the shop's door chimed and a customer walked in.

"Hector?" Grazia called again

through the door gap, more urgently this time.

"Hello," the customer said to her with a smile.

"Hello." She smiled back tensely.

If this man was one of the people who had left anxious messages on Hector's answering machine yesterday, she had better prepare to assuage him.

"I've come to collect a jacket I left with your husband about a week ago," the man said.

Your husband?

Would these words have rocked her as much if she hadn't had that dream?

Explaining that she wasn't Hector's wife, nor his employee, but she was authorised to peer through the door to his flat and call his name—which was how the man had found her—would be embarrassing both for her and for the customer.

"I'll call him down," she said to the man.

Grazia called Hector's name louder. There was a rumble down the stairs then Hector appeared, unshaven and with red-rimmed eyes. He must have had another bad night.

"Hi. This gentleman here would

like to collect his jacket."

"As I told your wife, I left it last week," the man repeated. "It needed a minor alteration."

Grazia was dismayed. She should have corrected the man earlier, before the husband-wife thing cropped up again. Now Hector was looking stricken.

How many times must his real wife have been in the shop when he was upstairs? No doubt she had received customers and had called him down when he was required. What had just happened must have given him the saddest déjà vu.

"I'm sorry, I'm not his wife," Grazia admitted, then hastily corrected herself. "That is, I'm sorry that I didn't correct you earlier. I'm not sorry that I'm not his wife!"

She was making it a lot worse. Heat crept up her cheeks.

Hector went to the cupboard, pulled out a garment and handed it to the man.

"Here is your jacket. It's ready"

The customer tried the jacket on, Hector packed it up again, the man paid and left the shop. All the while, Grazia didn't dare move. She was feeling like an imposter and an

intruder. If Hector had been hurt, it was her fault.

CHAPTER 24

"I've almost finished the wedding dress," Hector said, avoiding her gaze.

"When did you do that?"

He had only just started it when they said goodbye yesterday.

"I worked late."

This explained the unshaven

cheeks and the red-rimmed eyes.

"You shouldn't work at night."

"Why?"

Because she hated thinking he was driving himself into the ground.

"It's bad for your eyes and you could make mistakes. A mistake on a wedding dress is unacceptable," she said instead.

He stiffened. "I made no mistakes."

Oh, no, she had offended him.

"Now I can resume your dress for the wedding," he said.

Which wasn't a wedding dress. Memories of her dream flashed back. She wasn't meant to marry Hector!

She was to meet The One at Rebecca's wedding.

"Good, because that dress is really important. At Rebecca's wedding I'm going to meet my future husband," she told him.

A flick of his eyebrows betrayed Hector's surprise. "Have you been set up with someone?"

"No, but I know that I'm going to meet The One there. I feel the time is right."

"I gather it's to be a small wedding."

"Love can always find a way."

"Rather than love, it sounds more

like divination," Hector commented.

"I will not let you be disparaging about a matter so close to my heart. I've waited fifty years for The One."

"Sorry."

He looked contrite but his words still hurt. He didn't believe her. He thought her crazy.

"Let's get to work. I'll fetch Rebecca's dress."

He plodded to the back of the shop.

Grazia threaded her needles and started the hem of another pair of trousers. She finished it and Hector still wasn't back. She slid off her stool and went over to the cupboard where he was rummaging.

"I can't find the dress," he told her.

"Where did you last see it?"

"Here. I put it in this cupboard last night before I went to bed."

"Is it possible that you were too tired to remember and you put it somewhere else?"

He scowled. "I do not walk about my workshop with wedding dresses in my hands and leave them lying about in the wrong places."

"Fine, then it has to be here."

Grazia opened the cupboard door more fully. Inside were trousers, suits and other garments in various stages of repair or construction. Nothing remotely white.

Panic rose inside her.

"I'm sorry to insist, but you must have put it somewhere else without realising. This is why you shouldn't work late into the night," she added.

"I did not put it somewhere else!"

He gave her a less-than-friendly look then walked away and rummaged inside another cupboard. Then another.

Grazia's panic mounted. Rebecca was going through a lot of obstacles to be back in time for her wedding. If she managed to make it home after all the difficulties, she had better not be forced to cancel her wedding because she had no dress.

"I can't understand! I put it in this cupboard last night. I'll ask the girls if they've seen it."

He disappeared up the stairs to the flat while Grazia sat back on her stool.

CHAPTER 25

Why was Hector taking so long? Had he still not found Rebecca's dress? Surely it had to be somewhere inside the shop or in the flat. Thieves didn't steal wedding dresses, did they?

Nervous, Grazia swung her legs back and forth, hard and harder. She wound the stool round and round, higher and higher until she was perched so high that she couldn't get down. She was stuck!

She heard footsteps coming down the stairs and, for a moment, imagined that the urgency was in order to rescue her from her high perch.

The pallor of Hector's face, however, told her that his sudden haste was due to bad news.

"What happened?" she asked.

He looked at her as though he barely saw her. "Ella and George have run away."

"What? I don't understand."

The stool wobbled under her.

"They've eloped. And they've taken the dress with them." Hector let out a long, slow breath as if to steady himself.

Grazia felt like she might topple off the stool altogether.

"Did you scold them the night of the party?" she asked. "Did you forbid them to see each other again?"

"No, not at all."

"Then why would they do this?"

"I don't know."

He ran a hand over his face. The poor man looked like he had been hit by an emotional hurricane and was still reeling and swaying.

Grazia wanted to take his hand and squeeze it, to comfort him in some way, but she was trapped on her perch. "We have to find them. Where could they have gone?"

He shrugged. "I have no idea. Nor do Ella's sisters. I just found this note."

He handed her a piece of paper that clearly had been torn from a notebook. Then he leaned against the wall as she scanned the note.

"Daddy, I'm sorry but George and I have gone to get married. I've got to

take my life into my own hands. I've borrowed a wedding dress I found in your workshop. I'll bring it back as soon as I'm done with it. Ella x."

"We must get the dress back!" Grazia cried.

Hector narrowed his eyes at her. "Actually, I don't feel that's the biggest problem here."

"But it is! It sounds like Ella has no idea that the wedding dress belongs to her mother-in-law. If she gets married in it and finds out later..."

"What would be so wrong with that?"

Grazia shuddered at the thought.

"I would cringe. I would absolutely hate it!"

Hector still looked confused.

"Let's go to Rebecca's house and see if George has left any clues as to where they are," she suggested.

"That's a good idea."

He started towards the door, but Grazia couldn't follow.

"Can you help me down from this stool?"

He blinked.

"Could I have a hand, please?"

He rushed back to her and she leaned on his arm and climbed down. She followed him to the back door and out the back of the shop and into his car.

"I thought you approved of George," she questioned as they travelled towards Rebecca's house.

"I do, but eighteen is too early to get married," he replied.

"Not if you've found The One," Grazia said, not without a prick of envy. Lucky Ella.

"They could have dated for now. Waited until they were a little older, had completed their education and got jobs," Hector replied.

"They wouldn't be the first to make irrational choices guided by lust," Grazia told him, then regretted it. Ella was his daughter. That emotion was probably something Hector didn't want to think about.

"You are right. Nevertheless many people have indulged in lust without it resulting in marriage."

"Isn't that worse?" she challenged.

"To be honest I'm not sure."

"You want to stop them getting married, then?"

"Yes, and I think you should, too. I'm certain that's what Rebecca will ask you to do once you tell her."

"I'm not going to tell her! She has enough on her plate and she's far away. What can she possibly do?"

"So it's up to you to stop George doing anything he might regret later."

She nodded. "I will. I'm on your team."

"Great. I doubted that for a moment."

He was right. She had focused on stopping Ella from using Rebecca's wedding dress. She hadn't seen anything wrong in George and Ella marrying. Wasn't marrying a nice man what all women wanted, after all?

She hadn't considered their

parents' point of view. The couple were still young and probably hadn't thought things through.

When they got to Rebecca's house, Grazia noticed that the car was missing from the drive.

"If they've taken the car, I guess they haven't gone to our village vicar to get married," she decided.

"Of course not. He would have told me at once."

"We should call the police," Grazia suggested.

"They're legally adults and they've left of their own accord," Hector pointed out. "I doubt we can ask the police to find them and bring them home."

That meant she and Hector were going to have to do that.

CHAPTER 26

It was a school holiday and Luke and Leo were not out of bed yet when Grazia and Hector let themselves into the house with Grazia's key.

The boys were shocked to hear that their brother had eloped—though it wasn't clear that they knew what eloping meant. Certainly they had no idea where the couple might have gone.

"I know the password of George's laptop," Luke suggested. "He uses his laptop more than his phone. I guess we could check his browser history."

"That's a great idea," Hector said, looking brighter.

"Have you told Mum?" Leo asked Grazia.

"Not yet. She's got a lot of worries at the moment, being stuck, and there's nothing she can do from where she is. Hector and I are going to search for George and

Ella. Hopefully we can stop them before they've taken any big steps. You might want to tell your father, though. You can give him my number if he wants to know more."

Leo snorted disparagingly. "Our dad couldn't care less."

Grazia felt a pang of sympathy. She knew how that felt. Her own late father had not been a loving and caring presence in her life. He had been physically present, granted, but not with love.

"Look!" Hector pointed to the laptop's screen, which showed the website of a flower shop. "That will be the wedding bouquet."

How romantic, Grazia thought, that even though they were eloping and probably had little to no money, George had still made sure that Ella would have a bouquet.

"Oh, no, the shop is miles away!"

Hector's voice pulled her out of her reverie.

"Where is it?"

"In London."

"Why so far? That makes no sense."

"We used to live in London," Luke offered.

The rest of George's online search

history was related to schoolwork. There were no other clues.

The next moment, Grazia and Hector were back in the car, headed for the little flower shop in London.

The car's cosy interior had become so familiar to Grazia that she wasn't afraid of the road anymore.

"I still don't understand why they've done it," Hector mourned. "What has pushed Ella to go behind my back like this?"

"She did leave you a letter and she apologised."

"That means that she loves me. Not that I'm a good father and she felt she could talk to me."

"But you are a good dad," Grazia protested.

"If that were true, Ella would have told me she wanted to marry George. I thought there were no secrets between us."

"I'm sorry."

She put a hand over the arm he kept on the gearstick. The gesture felt familiar and, for a moment, she imagined being a family with Hector and the girls.

"Maybe she thought you would try to stop her, which you are doing, after all. It doesn't mean that she doesn't love you, and even less that you are a bad father."

"You know, you're a lot nicer than you let on," Hector replied, smiling slightly.

CHAPTER 27

"Whoever you choose to marry, you must learn to forgive:

It's the obligatory step for love to flourish and live."

—From the Sicilian Mama's "How to Pick a Husband" blog.

"I heard there are many Italians in London," Hector said as he

took the slip road marked M4 East.

"I don't know and I don't care."

He glanced at her. "If I've offended you, I'm sorry."

"You haven't. I just don't like being reminded that I'm different. Besides, why would I want to mix with other Italians? It wouldn't help me become a real British woman."

He frowned. "What's a 'real' British woman? Britons come in all shapes and sizes."

"The absence of an accent would be a start. In Calcotbury shopkeepers who don't know me ask me where I'm visiting from."

"British accents come in all kinds, too. The villagers would count you as a visitor if you had an accent of another part of the UK."

"They wouldn't need to ask, though."

"Differences make people interesting. Your Italianness adds variety, and variety is the spice of life. You can be the spice of Calcotbury!"

"No, thanks." Grazia shook her head. "Some spices don't blend in."

"Is that what you want?"

"I want to be so normal that I'm invisible."

Hector turned and looked at her.

"I don't think you could ever be invisible."

He smiled at her with a tenderness that suggested he didn't mean that she was too large or too loud. Nobody had ever looked at her like that.

He had to look away as the campervan in front of them used the brakes. There was a jam ahead and they were stuck between the campervan and a slow truck. This journey might keep them away from Hector's workshop for longer than he could spare.

She was sad for that as he might lose some custom, but she was happy for herself. She enjoyed talking to Hector. She could tell him things she had never put into words or told anyone. He didn't judge her and he seemed interested.

"I think your accent is lovely," he went on. "My grandfather had an accent. None of us ever thought of mocking him about it. It was the way he spoke; we didn't know him any other way. We loved it because that was him."

"But there's my name as well—Grazia Colonna. A dead giveaway. At least when I marry I'll have a British surname," she said.

"Is having a British surname non-negotiable for The One?"

"Not non-negotiable, but preferable."

She remembered Hector had a Spanish surname. But he wasn't The One. The One was...

She searched her brain for all the characteristics that she'd attributed to this mythical figure, but her mind was blank. The One had disappeared from her memory, to be replaced by Hector. He filled her brain.

Wait! This man wasn't right for her for innumerable reasons, even if, this instant, she couldn't think of a single one. The more she tried to dismiss him the more she wanted him to love her as fiercely as he loved his daughters.

"What are the non-negotiable requisites?" he asked. "Do you have a checklist or will you just know when you meet him? How can you be sure he will be at Rebecca's wedding?"

"So many questions. Why do you want to know?" A little glimmer of hope—inappropriate, senseless and crazy—flickered in her chest. She squashed it. "You're clearly not The One," Grazia said firmly, as much to herself as to him.

"Right, I'm not."

"You're not," she repeated as if to convince herself further.

Suddenly the clouds were greyer, the fields a little less green and the motorway a little less safe.

She took a deep breath.

"I mean, I'm the one who should be asking you questions. You've fallen in love, got married and had children. I know nothing about all these things, while clearly you know a lot," she explained.

He laughed bitterly. "I know nothing, especially about parenting! My daughter has just eloped and I had no idea."

Grazia wanted to say something soothing and encouraging. All that came to mind was that Ella had found The One and she hadn't even had to wait! Hector should be happy for her!

She knew that wasn't going to cut it.

CHAPTER 28

They drove in silence for the rest of the way. Grazia fell asleep for a bit, only waking up when they got off the motorway. She had never fallen asleep in the presence of a man. Another first.

She checked the vanity mirror for any dribble marks on her chin.

Thankfully there were none. She looked out of the window. They were driving through a suburb of London.

"I recognise this area," she said.

"I believe this is where Rebecca and the boys lived before moving to Calcotbury," Hector told her.

"That's right! I see now—it all makes perfect sense."

"What does?"

"George has behaved like the salmons. He has gone back to the river where he was spawned in order to spawn again."

"If it's all the same to you, I don't like the idea of Ella and George ‘spawning’.”

“Sorry.”

They stopped at a traffic light. She stole a look at Hector. “I thought all parents looked forward to becoming grandparents.”

“Ella and George are only eighteen,” he replied.

“Perhaps you don’t like the idea of becoming a grandparent because it ages you. Besides, as you’re probably looking for a new wife...”

“I am not looking for a new wife,” he interrupted.

She felt a pang of disappointment. Perhaps it was just because of the brusqueness of his interruption.

"My daughter is only eighteen," he went on more calmly. "I don't want her to spawn before she's even chosen her career path."

"I'm sorry. You must understand that my own mother was eighteen when she had me. Still, you're right—having me certainly hasn't been the highlight of her life."

"Why do you say that?"

"For one thing, she keeps calling me 'Disgrazia', which means misfortune, and she keeps reminding me that I'm her misfortune," Grazia observed.

Hector shook his head.

"That contradicts the fact that she keeps you on such a short leash."

"I'm not on a leash!" Grazia protested.

"Of course you are. You need to ask permission to leave her, she demands to know where you go and for how long, she wants you back at set times and rings you if you're late. You're not even allowed to take your own clothes to the tailor," he concluded.

Thinking about it, Grazia realised Hector was right. She was on a leash, and a short one at that.

She was too proud to admit it,

though. "Nonsense. She's just an Italian mother."

"Grazia, you must be careful not to use your Italian identity as a scapegoat for things that don't work as they should."

So judgment had arrived. It had only been a matter of time. Hector was like everyone else who judged her for the way she let Rosaria treat her.

"Stop the car! I'm getting out." She pulled on the door handle.

"I'm sorry to have upset you."

Hector sounded genuinely sorry, but his apology couldn't stop the tide of shame, anger and upset that was rising in Grazia's heart.

"I must get out! Please, stop the car."

He pulled over and she shot out of the car. He drove off.

She marched along the pavement, every step like trying to stamp out a fire. She strode on, long after Hector's car had disappeared, until her heart was under control again.

Yes, he had judged her and no doubt he thought her stupid. A dupe. A mug. But could they put their differences of opinions aside and work together to rescue George, Ella and Rebecca's wedding dress? Could they be friends again? If they ever had been friends.

Most importantly, would he return for her? She had only twenty pounds in her wallet, no cards, a phone that was no smarter than herself and a packet of salted crackers for sustenance.

The best course of action was to swallow her pride and ring him, begging him to take her back. She picked up her phone and rang his number.

It rang and rang. Was he not picking up because he was driving or because he was mad at her? Both options were plausible.

She realised she could hear his phone ringing both through her phone and outside.

"Grazia, I'm over here."

Hector's voice came from behind some bushes. On the other side of them, she saw, was a car park. He hadn't abandoned her after all.

CHAPTER 29

Relief and gratitude flooded her.

"Hector, I'm sorry."

"I'm sorry, too. We've no time to squabble. Let's go."

He helped her step through a sparse section of the hedge. The car park belonged to a shopping complex containing a hairdresser, baker, hardware store and carpet shop.

"What are we doing here?" she asked, doubling her steps to keep up with Hector's long strides.

"Visiting the florist."

The shop was stocked with anemones, dahlias and peonies. There were flowers that Grazia didn't even know existed. They were so perfect that, if they hadn't been standing in vases of water, she would have thought they were made of silk.

This was a different world from the supermarkets where carnations, lilies and roses thrived. It was a kingdom of muted colours, vintage bottles and retro candles.

A beautiful young woman with curls escaping from a flowery snood was behind the counter, working with pliers and metal wire. Grazia wished she, too, could be young and beautiful, working in a florist shop instead of Rosaria's Pantry.

"Good morning. I believe that you've been given the wrong delivery address for a wedding bouquet," Hector told the young woman.

The woman put down the pliers and wire. "Oh, dear. What's the name?"

"Gonzales."

She reached for her tablet and tapped away with the tips of her fingers, which escaped from her fingerless gloves. "Ibis hotel, Lakeshore View?"

"Ah, I see. Actually, that was the right address. Sorry, my mistake," he said.

The woman let out a breath. "Thank goodness, because the delivery girl said that the bouquet had been delivered. All's well, then?"

"Yes, thank you. Goodbye."

"What was that all about? How did you know which address was correct?" Grazia asked him after they'd left the shop.

He smiled. "I didn't. I was bluffing. I guessed that George had ordered a wedding bouquet and I wanted the girl to tell me where she had delivered it because that might tell us where the church was. Unfortunately they didn't get it delivered to the church but to a hotel. What I think is that they've booked the hotel for tonight and they probably used it to get dressed for the wedding," Hector explained. "It makes sense that they would have the bouquet delivered there. A girl in a wedding dress will not go unnoticed. I'm hoping that the hotel staff will be able to give us some clues." He checked his watch. "I just hope we're not too late," he muttered.

They got caught in traffic. Hector rapped his fingers on the steering wheel. "These two couldn't have chosen a worst time to pull this stunt on us. You've a deli to open and I have Rebecca's wedding dress and your dress to finish, plus all the daily work."

Grazia tried to lighten the mood. "Look on the bright side. If George and Ella have organised their own wedding, you haven't had to spend a penny on it!"

He gave her a strange look.

The hotel was on a noisy dual carriageway. The desk was unmanned so Hector pressed a bell. A grumpy-looking teenager emerged from a backdoor, chewing gum.

"Hello. We have a message for some of your guests—the couple getting married today," Hector told him.

"I don't know who you're talking about," the girl drawled.

"Have you seen a girl leave the hotel in a wedding dress?" Grazia pressed.

"No. I've only just started my shift."

"Could you look them up on your list, please? George Lewis and Ella Gonzales," Hector said.

"We don't offer full concierge service. Passing messages on to guests is not within the remit of my job," the girl replied.

"Could you tell us where they've gone so we can deliver the message ourselves, then?" Grazia asked.

The girl shook her ponytail. "I would be breaching privacy and data protection laws. Also, I don't know

anything. If you've lost your children, you need to contact the police."

CHAPTER 30

They walked out of the hotel, despondent. George's car wasn't parked there, they saw.

Hector tried again to ring Ella's mobile and George's but, unsurprisingly, they weren't answering.

"Let's think. Why would they come

all the way to London to get married?" Grazia asked.

"Please, spare me the salmon-spawning theory."

"What I mean is, where would they go in London? Why here?"

"To make it harder for us to find them and stop them, no doubt," Hector replied. "They would hardly ask our village vicar to do the deed."

"Yes, but they could have gone to another city like Bristol, Gloucester or Swindon. They've come here because this is George's home ground. He grew up here." She stopped herself mentioning the spawning salmon again.

"If we want to find them, we need to think like them," she continued. "Where would George go to get married? Somewhere he's familiar with, where he could enlist the help of someone who knows him." She gasped. "Did they attend any church when they were living here?"

They rang the boys at home.

"Yes, we did go to church every now and then. We were baptised there."

Luke described where it was—only a few streets away from the florist. Grazia and Hector dived back into the car and drove to the church. Hector launched himself out of the car and she ran after him.

The church was empty.

“We’re too late!”

Hector sank onto a kneeler with his head in his hands. “Where did I go wrong? I tried my best to be a good father, to give my daughters everything they needed,” he muttered. He was crumbling.

Grazia stroked his back comfortingly. “Maybe our guesses were wrong and they haven’t been here. We might be still in time. Let’s talk to the vicar.”

Hector heaved himself up from the pew. “Thank you. I don’t know what I’d do without you by my side.”

The vicarage was joined to the church and the vicar answered the door promptly.

“I was expecting you,” he told them. “Come in, Mr and Mrs Gonzales.”

“Mrs Gonzales”. The name didn’t feel as wrong to Grazia as she had imagined. Though clearly not British, it felt good. Not despite its exotic ring but, perhaps, because of it. But it didn’t belong to her.

“I’m not Mrs Gonzales. I’m

George's guardian while his mother is away."

"George is an adult. There are no guardians," the vicar pointed out gently.

"In their parents' eyes George and Ella are still kids," she argued.

"Please tell us you haven't married them," Hector begged.

"To be exact, it is not the celebrant who marries a couple. It's the couple who marry each other. That is the sacrament," the vicar explained.

He seemed in no hurry to answer. Grazia's heart sank. It must already be too late.

"Are George and Ella now man and wife?" she asked.

"No. They changed their mind."

CHAPTER 31

"If your family is holding you back,

Break the shackle and go on your track."

—From the Sicilian Mama's "How to Pick a Husband" blog.

"Thank God!" Hector cried.

"What do you mean

they changed their mind?" Grazia asked.

"I was ready, waiting for them, but this morning they called and told me they had changed their mind. The wedding was off. I have no idea why," the vicar said.

"And I have no idea why they would think of getting married in the first place!" Hector complained.

"Perhaps you need to communicate more with your child. Problems arise when parents are too busy to listen to their children."

Hector's nostrils flared.

"I have children, too," the vicar

went on. "Sometimes we let our jobs get in the way of family life and we don't make time to listen."

"I listen to my daughters all the time! I work downstairs from our flat and they know they can come in and talk to me whenever I'm on my own —which is most of the time. I spend my days sitting in my workshop on my own, with needle and thread in my hand, practically a sitting target for all my daughters' needs!" Hector protested.

"I'm sure that there's always scope for improvement," the vicar argued gently.

"Do you know where they might be now?" Grazia tried to keep to the point.

"Are they on their way home?" Hector added.

"No. They don't want to go home."

"Why not?" Hector asked, upset.

"Where are they?" Grazia was eager to get the information before Hector blew his top.

"They mentioned visiting some friends."

"But where?" Grazia asked.

The vicar sighed. "I shouldn't be telling you but, as I say, I'm a parent, too." He scribbled an address on a piece of paper and handed it to them. "I didn't tell you anything. You found it."

"Understood. Thank you!"

They returned to the car.

"Look on the bright side—" she began, but Hector interrupted her.

"Please, don't."

"They haven't got married."

He grunted, but she knew she was right.

His daughter had tried to get married, didn't want to go home and other people knew this while he was in the dark. Still, Ella was unmarried.

Grazia felt tender towards Ella.

Protective. Almost parental. Was this how it felt? It was too late for the joy of motherhood, but might she experience the joy of being a step-mother?

"What time will we be back home?" Grazia asked.

Hector flicked the indicator and turned into yet another residential road.

"I have no idea. It depends on when we manage to find my daughter and your charge. To be honest, I haven't thought that far."

Oh, no! Dinnertime was her curfew. "Will you leave your

daughters alone at home overnight?"

"Yes. They're old enough to look after themselves for one night, and they can turn to our neighbours if they have a problem. Would it be a problem for you to spend the night away, if needed?"

"Yes."

He considered. "If your mother needs help with meals or getting ready for bed, I know someone who could come and help her."

"No need. She's perfectly able to do all these things. It's just, I can't tell her I won't be coming home tonight. I've never done it before." Warmth crept up her cheeks.

He was considerate enough not to show surprise nor ask questions about school trips (she was never allowed), trips with friends (even more forbidden) or any other legitimate reasons a woman might have to spend a night away from home. Nor did he ask why she had never rebelled.

"Would it be okay if I dropped you off at a train station if it starts to look like things won't be sorted tonight?"

She checked her watch. "Yes, but I've got to get home before dinnertime, around five-thirty."

"I'm not sure you could make it back before then even if there was a direct train and a taxi at the other end. Can't you ask your mother to have supper a little later?"

Grazia squirmed. "Not really."

It sounded ridiculous that she couldn't call home and tell Rosaria that supper would have to be a little later. That she was free to go ahead and have supper without her. But Grazia had seen the suspicion in Rosaria's eyes when she had negotiated this day out. Arriving late or postponing supper would set Rosaria on her like a bloodhound.

How could this happen? When she had negotiated with Rosaria her time off until supper, it had felt like ages. Almost an entire day of freedom! Now it felt like it had flown by.

"Does your mother need pills at set times?" Hector was trying to understand the issue.

"I need to make a phone call," Grazia said, not responding to this.

"By all means," he said without stopping the car.

She had hoped he would let her out of the car so she could talk in private, but that was silly—they didn't have time to stop. Also, there were double lines on the side of the road. Even without knowing the Highway Code she could guess that it wasn't a good thing.

There was only one thing she could do to save herself embarrassment: talk to her mother in Italian.

She hadn't done this with her mother since her teenage years, both as a small act of rebellion and to accelerate her transformation into a full British woman. She picked up her phone and rang the landline.

CHAPTER 32

No answer. This wasn't siesta time. Why wasn't Rosaria picking up?

"I think my mother is in trouble! She's not answering the phone."

"Maybe she can't hear it," Hector reasoned. "She might be out."

"She doesn't go out when I'm not

at home."

"Try again."

Grazia tried Rosaria's mobile this time.

"Hello?" Rosaria answered.

"Here you are! How are you?" Grazia asked, forgetting to speak in Italian.

"Very well. Why?"

"You didn't answer the landline."

"Hasn't it occurred to you that I might not be at home? Why are you ringing?" Rosaria asked with a hint of accusation.

Grazia swallowed and braced herself for her mother's wrath. "I'm not sure I can make it back for dinner. Can we have it later?"

"Is that all? You called me for that?"

"Well, yes."

The last time Grazia had been late for dinner Rosaria had rung the police!

"You shouldn't have disturbed me. Do whatever you want; I don't care."

Grazia heard a man's voice in the background. "Who's that?" he asked.

"Just my silly daughter." Rosaria answered the man without bothering to cover the phone's receiver.

"Don't ever disturb me again for

such silliness, Disgrazia. Rupert and I are playing cards and he's winning, so I can't afford to take my eyes off him. Am I right, naughty boy?" She giggled coquettishly.

What? Grazia had fretted over this phone call, imagining her mother sitting by the phone waiting for her return. Meanwhile, Rosaria was playing cards and flirting with the antiques dealer!

"So you don't need me to come back and cook you dinner?"

"Whatever for? I can cook better than you! Now, if you'll leave us alone..."

Rosaria was about to end the call but Grazia jumped in.

"What about tonight? Do you need me back?"

"Disgrazia, you're being a pain and I'm busy. Do whatever you want and leave me in peace. Goodbye."

Grazia was stunned. She had worried herself sick about Rosaria's reaction, yet it turned out that not only did she not care a fig about her daughter, but she didn't need her, either.

All these years since her father's death, Grazia's mother had wanted her by her side only because she had no one else. She had never cared for Grazia, who had only been a plug for her solitude, second best to her father and now to Rupert. Rosaria's love had only ever been for herself.

"Is your mother okay?" Hector asked.

"She is. So well that I'm not going to take a train home tonight. I'll stay with you until we've found George and Ella."

"Good."

Was he pleased because he liked her company or because he wouldn't have to make a detour to the train station?"

"I didn't want to say, but I didn't like the idea of having to face my daughter without you."

A warm glow spread over Grazia at these words. Nobody had ever made her feel so valued. Certainly not Rosaria.

CHAPTER 33

The flat of those friends of George seemed to be in another country to Hector and Grazia. The evening rush hour had turned the roads into gridlock.

"We need more fuel," Grazia decided.

"If we stop for fuel, we'll waste

precious time."

"If we run out of fuel and have to continue on foot, we'll waste even more time, Hector. Anyway, we know that they aren't about to get married. Even if they changed their mind again, the vicar would be unlikely to agree to marry them tonight. And, I should hope, he would call us first."

He agreed to stop for petrol and she insisted on paying half. She also picked up a few snacks, given that they had skipped lunch and there were no plans for supper.

They snacked on crisps and chocolate buttons in the car. Grazia dropped the food into the palm of Hector's hand and he would toss it into his mouth.

"George's car!" Grazia cried at last with relief.

They could reasonably assume that George and Ella were inside one of the flats, but which one? There were twelve doorbells.

"We'll just have to ring them all," Hector told her.

For their first three tries there was no answer. After that, each time someone answered the intercom he introduced himself as Ella's dad and asked if she was there. But nobody seemed to know her or George.

"Maybe Ella is hiding from me and she has told George's friend to tell us that she's not there," he fretted with his finger hovering over the intercom bell of the last remaining flat.

Grazia took his other hand and squeezed it. "We'll sit in the car until either of them comes out the front door, then we'll beg them to talk to us."

He smiled, nodded and pressed the last intercom.

"Oh, yeah, bro. She's here. Come up."

And just like that, they were

buzzed in.

"Up" wasn't a very helpful direction, as it turned out.

"As we don't know which floor they are on, we'll have to take the stairs," Hector told her, heading for the stairs. The knowledge that Ella was in the building and wasn't hiding from him seemed to have reinvigorated him.

Grazia felt reinvigorated too, but she would still rather have taken the lift up to the top floor and walked down to the required floor! Unfortunately Hector was already pounding up the stairs and there was no way Grazia wouldn't be by his side when he confronted his daughter.

Up until this morning, she had wanted to be with him because he made her feel happier, safer and valued. Now, she realised, she wanted to be with him so that she could make *him* feel happier, safer and valued.

By the second floor she was out of breath, yet still no door was opening for them.

It was only when they got to the fifth floor, panting and wiping their brows, that a door opened.

There stood Ella and George, looking very contrite but, Grazia

noticed with relief, holding hands.

Clearly, even if the wedding was off, their relationship wasn't.

CHAPTER 34

"I'm sorry, Dad!" Ella ran into his arms.

This left Grazia and George looking at each other awkwardly, because there was no way George would run into her arms or her into his.

"Why did you do this?" Hector

asked his daughter. "I never prevented you from dating George."

"It's not about George; it's about home. That's one reason why we've called it off. When we do get married, we'll do it for each other, not to escape our home lives."

"When" not "if", Grazia noted.

"Escape your home life? Why?"

"Dad, since Mum passed away you've expected me to look after my sisters as if I was her, but I'm not their mother. You hold me responsible for them. It's unfair and it drains me of the energy I need to get on with my studies, with my life."

Hector was ashen. “I didn’t realise. I’m so sorry.”

“It’s not your fault. You were floundering too. We were all thrown off balance when Mum passed. Now I need to think about my own future. I said I didn’t want to go to university because I felt guilty at leaving you alone. I thought that, if I got married, I wouldn’t feel guilty about leaving you. That’s not a good reason to get married, though.”

Hector hugged her tighter.

“What about you, George? Did you want to leave your home too?” Grazia asked.

"Yes. I don't want Charles to become my stepdad."

"Does your mother know how you feel about it?"

"No. It's her life and she can do what she wants with it—I have no right to stop her remarrying. I just wanted out before that happened. But I guess that's not a good reason to get married. Also, having a proper wedding with guests and a party would be nicer. I would have gone through with it today, but when I saw Ella in the wedding dress and recognised it was Mum's, it was too cringy. I couldn't marry her in that dress."

Ella's hands flew to her chest. "I had no idea! I was horrified when George told me. I will never steal anything from your shop again, Dad."

"Good to know." Hector nodded. "Listen, marriage should never be used as an escape. It brings its own challenges and pitfalls. It's never an easy way out."

Grazia was surprised at this.

"What made you decide to do it now?" he asked. "Because I told you off for not watching your sisters at the party?"

Ella twisted the hem of her

cardigan around her fingers and looked at her feet. George came to her rescue.

"For me it was Mum being away and her wedding coming up. I felt it was now or never."

Ella looked up. "I follow a blog by someone called 'The Sicilian Mama'. This week she posted 'If your family is holding you back, break the shackle and go on your track'. It felt like she was talking to me."

"She wasn't!" Grazia protested.

"You know the blog? Do you follow her too?" Ella asked.

"Yes," Grazia replied, feeling her

cheeks warm.

"She's great, isn't she?"

"No, she's not. She's an idiot," Grazia replied.

"I'm sorry, Ella, I won't ask so much of you anymore," Hector said. "You must promise that the next time you have a problem, a grievance, you will talk to me. Don't just run away."

Ella hugged him again. "I'm sorry, Dad, I didn't mean to hurt you. You are a wonderful dad and you've done a great job looking after us on your own. Don't let my actions make you think otherwise."

"I've made mistakes too. It's been

very hard for us all since your mother passed away and I've asked too much of you."

George scratched the back of his head. "I'm sorry, Grazia, if I put you in a tight spot."

"It's okay." Grazia knew how it felt to wish she could run away from home. "I haven't told your mother anything yet. We could go home and leave her none the wiser, but I think it would be wrong. Even if she's still going to marry Charles, she needs to know how you feel."

George nodded. "I will tell her everything, I promise."

With two days' worth of stubble, a few nights of insufficient sleep, plus all the driving and the stress and worry of that day, Hector looked extremely tired.

Grazia felt sorry for him. He had two more daughters to look after and, now he'd promised to ease the load on his eldest, he'd have to work harder.

"I think we should go home now," she said.

Everyone agreed. Unfortunately the wedding dress had been left in the hotel.

Hector told George and Ella to

return home while he and Grazia would go back to the hotel with the room key and pick up the dress.

The bodice that Hector had only got as far as basting had splayed opened when Ella had worn it. There was no way Hector would be able to finish Rebecca's wedding dress and Grazia's dress before the wedding. She would have to wear another, less flattering dress out of her cupboard.

She found she didn't care about her dress anymore, about looking her best at Rebecca's wedding or about meeting The One.

She felt nothing but indifference

about that mythical man. Not even resentment for having kept her waiting. The One was no more than the poster of a pop idol. She had grown out of him.

Instead, there was a real man, living and breathing, loving and hurting, sitting in the driving seat next to her.

"You must be very tired," Grazia remarked softly. "If I could drive, I would offer to share the driving."

"I'll take you up on your offer as soon as you get your licence." Hector smiled.

At first she thought he was joking,

but his tone suggested he wasn't. He believed that she wasn't too old, too clumsy, too distracted or stupid to learn to drive if she wanted to.

"You can sleep, if you like. There's a cushion on the back seat if you want to reach out and grab it," he offered.

"Thanks but I don't feel sleepy."

Happy moments weren't made for sleeping through.

The lights of London glowed behind them and now the motorway was crossing dark countryside. Somewhere out there rabbits scratched in their warrens, foxes trotted across fields, badgers rubbed their coats against the trunks of trees. She was tucked in this cosy little car with Hector, the knight in shining armour who had rescued her and had been rescued by her, in some part.

He had been by her side from the moment she had sought his help with her dress, to that panicked night of the house party, then to today, when her best friend's wedding dress had gone missing together with her son.

Even now, as they barrelled down the motorway at seventy miles per hour into the darkness of the night, she felt safe.

CHAPTER 35

"Some of those you thought were on your side,

Never actually wanted you to be a bride."

—From the Sicilian Mama's "How to Pick a Husband" blog.

"I'll accompany you to your door. It's late," Hector stated.

Another time Grazia would have insisted that he drop her off at the end of the road out of sight from Rosaria. Today, though, her mother had shown that she didn't care—her attention was on Rupert.

Hector parked at the back of the deli and accompanied her up the dark stairs all the way to the door. She inserted the key into the lock and turned it.

"Thank you, Hector. Despite everything, it's been a good day." She didn't add "with you".

Her gaze fell on his lips and she wished he would kiss her. Then a light snapped on inside the flat behind her.

"Disgrazia! What do you think you're doing coming home at this time?"

She was startled but rallied. "You told me I could stay out all night so long as I left you and Rupert in peace."

"I'm not with Rupert right now," Rosaria said, removing her shoes.

She must have only just got home and realised that Grazia wasn't there to fill the void that Rupert had left. She hadn't been worried for Grazia, she was just irritated that there was no one to keep her company. Behind

Rosaria's jealousy and demands, Grazia realised, was fear of solitude.

Her mother noticed Hector on the stairs. "Who is this?"

"Hector Gonzales, the village tailor. You must be Grazia's mother," Hector replied in a tone that was polite but not warm.

Rosaria ignored him. "What does this mean?" she asked Grazia in Italian.

Possible answers flitted through Grazia's mind. She could say he was making tote bags and basket liners for their deli. She could even tell her that she and Hector were fixing

Rebecca's wedding dress.

But Grazia was fed up with a life of subterfuge, and Rosaria's words on the phone earlier still echoed in her mind.

"He's my friend," she answered in Italian.

"Friend? You don't have friends."

For years Grazia had justified Rosaria's put-downs in the name of love. It was out of love that Rosaria corrected her, pointed out her failings, kept her grounded and stopped her getting ideas above her station.

Now Grazia saw that this wasn't

true. Rosaria did these things so that Grazia wouldn't think herself capable of leaving. As she looked into her mother's eyes, she could see the fear behind the anger.

Rosaria's insistence that everyone disliked them for being Italian was another attempt to isolate her and keep her all for herself. The youths who had vandalised their restaurant had spray-painted "go home" on the door only after Rosaria had refused to serve them a takeaway.

Rosaria's heart had become so hard that she no longer knew the good from the bad. Right now she was scowling at Hector, one of the nicest men on earth. Instead of rejoicing that her daughter had a nice friend, she seemed to be trying to intimidate him. The only person Rosaria was capable of loving was herself.

"Hector is my good friend. We met when I gave him my dress to alter for the wedding," Grazia said in English, refusing to talk further in Italian. There was going to be no more secret language between her and Rosaria. No more "us against them".

"You gave him your dress? I told you not to!"

“It’s my dress and I can do what I want with it.”

Grazia’s voice was shaking with adrenaline. She had never defied Rosaria so openly. Amazingly the ground didn’t swallow her up and the sky didn’t send a lightning bolt to strike her.

“How dare you speak like that to your mother!” Rosaria cried.

Grazia turned to Hector. “You can go. You’ve had enough drama of your own today.”

He didn’t leave. He stood behind her like a protective wall. “I’ll stay until I know you’re safe,” he whispered.

The response touched her and filled her with courage. He understood that she wasn't safe with Rosaria. Even if Grazia was younger and stronger, Rosaria was nastier. If Hector was going to stand behind her until she was safe, he might never be able to leave.

"You're no longer my daughter! Leave this house!" Rosaria roared.

CHAPTER 36

Grazia reeled from the almost physical blow of the words.

In the past Rosaria had criticised her, mocked her and scolded her, but she had never chased her out of the house.

Grazia didn't know what to do. She had nowhere to go and not a penny to her name. Rosaria held all their money, owned the deli and kept all their paperwork filed away.

"Come to my place," Hector offered.

Fear flashed across Rosaria's eyes. This wasn't what she had hoped for. "You can't sleep at a man's house!"

In the past, Grazia would have reassured her that the house was filled with girls and that Hector would surely give her suitable accommodation.

"If I'm not your daughter, then I can do what I want," she said instead. She turned to Hector. "Thank you. I accept your offer. If you could wait a moment, I'll pack my bag."

"You're not packing anything! Everything you have belongs to me!" Rosaria shouted, but Grazia sidestepped her and strode towards her room.

Rosaria followed.

"You can't leave me! You can't go!" Rosaria cried, changing tack.

Grazia grabbed her nightdress and her toothbrush. She was about to take her laptop, but Rosaria snatched it from the table.

"You can't leave now!" she taunted.

"I can and I will," Grazia said and, dodging her, walked out.

"You can't leave!" Rosaria shouted from the top of the stairs.

Grazia was mortified. If the village wasn't already talking about George and Ella's elopement, it would surely be talking about the night-time quarrel of the newly arrived Italian women.

"You were very brave," Hector said as they drove towards his flat.

"Nobody has ever called me that," Grazia admitted.

"I think there will be many first times for you from now on."

***

Hector's flat was as messy as his shop, but had a feminine presence. Curling tongs lay plugged into the wall like another house might have a telephone. There were shoes everywhere, in every size from four to seven, with the occasional boat-sized pair that belonged to Hector.

As the girls heard their father opening the door, they appeared in a flurry of fluffy pink pyjamas and slippers.

"Daddy!" The youngest, Amanda, hugged Hector.

Ella was already there, looking

contrite.

"Hello." Amanda saw Grazia behind her dad. "Are you staying the night?"

"Yes."

"Wow! Daddy has a woman staying over!" Georgia told her sisters.

"Grazia will have my room and I'll sleep on the floor in your room," Hector explained.

A frisson either of excitement or fear ran down Grazia's back. She had never slept in a man's bed before. Would the linen smell of Hector—that delicious smell of old wood, new wool and sewing machine oil?

She imagined falling asleep with the scent of him in her nostrils. What dreams might come to her?

"Girls, make Grazia a cup of tea while I change the bedding," he told them.

That burst her bubble.

"What kind of tea?" Georgia asked.

Grazia opted for chamomile, hoping it would help her sleep despite the excitement of being in Hector's room and bed.

CHAPTER 37

The kitchen was cluttered with jars of tea infusions, cereal boxes and packets of biscuits. There was just enough space for the kettle on the counters.

Grazia wondered how they managed to do any food preparation, until she saw Georgia prepare her infusion by hovering the cup above the sink.

"Your bed is ready," Amanda announced from the kitchen door a moment later.

Grazia was escorted to the master bedroom. Hector had made up the bed with clean sheets and put a folded, clean towel at the foot of the bed. Among the chaos of the rest of the house, what he had made for her was a little island of tidiness.

"Thank you," she said gratefully.

He didn't leave immediately but watched her as she rounded the bed and placed her nightdress down on the left side of the bed.

"Have I done something wrong?" she asked as she saw him smile.

"You've chosen my wife's side of the bed, even though I put the towel on the other."

"Oh, I'm so sorry!"

"Don't be." He let his gaze linger on her and the room around her a little longer, as if he had checked how she fit in and was pleased with the result.

"If you need anything, let me know. Goodnight, Grazia."

"Goodnight, Hector. Thank you for your hospitality."

"My pleasure."

He closed the door and she slipped into her nightie and under the duvet. Her head sank into a pillow that smelled of fresh laundry and, yes, of Hector. She studied the room. What did it say about him?

No womanly traces were left. The flat was the girls' kingdom, but this was a man cave.

Books lined the shelves on the wall and a small desk with a computer was piled with men's tailoring magazines.

Tiredness crept in but, every time Grazia was about to drift off to sleep, the scent of Hector and the slope in the mattress that leaned towards the dip in his side of the bed kept her awake.

Hector was sleeping on the floor and she was gripped with guilt. Sleep would elude her unless she could reassure herself that he was comfortable.

She slipped out of bed, took a pillow and tiptoed out of the door. The flat was silent now. She passed the kitchen, the sitting room, the bathroom and reached the girls' room.

She stopped at the door. The gentle sound of snoring told her this was either a bear's cave or the place where Hector was sleeping.

She peered in and what she saw made her heart somersault in her chest.

Hector was lying on the floor between a bunk bed and a bed, his head resting on a rolled-up fluffy pink dressing gown and a Disney princess duvet stretched out over him in a pitiful attempt to cover his body. The three beds in the room were empty. Hector's daughters were on the floor with him, their heads on his chest, his arms protectively around them.

CHAPTER 38

A knock on the door woke Grazia up.

"We've made breakfast for you." Amanda proceeded into the room balancing a tray.

Nobody had ever done that for Grazia. Was this the way they had treated their mother when she was alive or was this a special treat for guests?

Whichever it was, Grazia was touched. “That’s very kind of you.”

Amanda smiled smugly, as if she had hoped for that reaction.

“What time is it? Have I overslept?”

“It’s only eight.”

“Is your dad awake?”

“He’s already in the shop working.”

“Oh, dear, I must get up!” Grazia said, leaping out of bed, then remembering that she was only in her tatty nightie.

“Nice nightie,” Amanda said. “It

reminds me of those ones in movies."

"Which movies?" Grazia asked.

"'Pride and Prejudice', 'Sense and Sensibility'—movies like that."

"I see."

Grazia got dressed as soon as Amanda had left, not just because she wanted to get out of her old-fashioned nightdress, but also to go down and help Hector.

She swallowed her tea in one gulp and stuffed toast in her mouth while putting on her tights and skirt.

To her surprise, when she got downstairs Hector wasn't working on Rebecca's dress but her own.

"Hi. Have you slept well?" he asked her kindly.

"I did, but I'm not sure you have," she said, smiling.

"I've slept very well."

Was he just being polite? Perhaps sleeping on the floor was more than compensated for by his daughters' hugs. How many fathers had three daughters who adored them like that? A longing to be part of that love welled inside her. There seemed to be plenty of love to go around in the Gonzales family.

"You don't have to work on my dress. Rebecca's is more important."

"I beg to disagree."

"But she's the bride! Of course her dress is more important than mine," Grazia argued.

"She has already found The One while you are looking for him at her wedding."

Grazia felt that she was looking at The One right now, even with his array of spectacles splayed on his head, a tape measure slung over his neck, and the eggcup-sized thimble on his finger.

There was no chance she could admit this to Hector, though. He wasn't interested in marrying again.

"If we put it that way then yes, my dress would be more important, I guess."

She took a stool on the opposite side of the worktable and started working on one of the many other garments on his to-do pile.

They worked in silence for what felt like ages, neither looking at each other.

A woman walked into the shop.

"Good morning, Mr Gonzales. I came by yesterday and you were closed," she said, more curious than offended.

"Yes, I'm sorry. I had urgent family

matters to attend to."

He stood up and opened the cupboard where he kept the finished garments ready for collection. It was almost empty and Grazia felt a pang of guilt because, had it not been for Rebecca's dress and all the other trouble she had brought on to him, he wouldn't be behind with his work.

"That's okay. I'm glad I had to make another trip into the village or I would never have discovered the new deli that's just opened," the woman told them.

"Just opened?" Grazia repeated in disbelief.

"Yes. Rosaria's Pantry, I think it's called. They're having an opening party."

Grazia felt a little stab through the ribs. So Rosaria was giving an opening party without her, no doubt to show her that she wasn't needed and that the delicatessen was nothing to do with her from this moment on.

Her mother had made it very clear last night that Grazia was no longer her daughter, but seeing her disowning in action still hurt.

"You could go over there now. The party is only just starting," the

customer reassured her.

Grazia forced a smile and managed to thank her.

The woman checked the repair to her husband's trousers, complimented the stitchwork—which had actually been Grazia's—then left the shop.

CHAPTER 39

"Are you okay?" Hector asked as soon as they were alone again.

"I suppose. It will take me a little time to get used to being out of Rosaria's life, but I'll get used to it."

"Any regrets?"

"None. I'm just shocked to discover

that she doesn't need me. I always believed that she couldn't manage without me."

He rounded the table, took the stool next to hers and held her hand. His hand was warm and soft. At his touch, life's spiky edges felt rounder and softer to her.

"If your mother can open the deli today it's because of all the hard work you've put in until now. She couldn't have done it without you," he said, then grew serious. "Have you got a share in the business?"

"No, everything belongs to her. She's within her rights to cut me out of it all."

"She will leave you without a livelihood?"

"Yes."

Just then, a courier walked into the shop and deposited a large box on the counter.

"For Mrs Gonzales," he said.

"There must be a mistake. She's deceased," Hector told him.

"I'm sorry, these are the instructions I was given. Mrs Gonzales. Signature here, please," the man added, thrusting a digital device at Hector.

Hector signed and the man left.

Who had sent a parcel to a woman who had been dead for five years? This would surely be upsetting for Hector.

Grazia joined him as he fetched a pair of scissors and started to open the box. Haphazardly tossed into the box were her own possessions. Her laptop, her clothes, shoes and even her toiletries!

He looked up at her with a question in his eyes and she nodded.

This parcel was Rosaria's way of cutting her off and also mocking her by addressing her with the title of Hector's wife.

"I'm sorry you've been dragged into this," she told him.

"Don't worry about me. You need to think about what you're going to do."

Yes, he was right. This parcel was her mother's way of telling her that last night hadn't been just another of their skirmishes. It was a permanent rupture from which she couldn't go back.

If this parcel hadn't arrived, would she have thought of crawling back to Rosaria, grovelling? No. Even if she had nowhere to live? No.

Now Hector seemed to be telling

her, kindly, that she shouldn't assume that she could stay with him permanently, even if she had no home anymore.

"Don't worry. I'll find somewhere to stay. If the boys don't mind, I could stay at Rebecca's until she returns."

That was if the fact that she turned up with a box containing all her possessions didn't scare them. "I'd just like a lift over there in the car, if you don't mind, so I can take my box."

"Stay with us," he replied.

It sounded like more than an invitation. A hope. A wish.

"Stay as long as you like," Hector added.

"I can't do that."

Because "as long as you like" would mean forever.

"You slept on the floor last night, I know it," she challenged.

"I don't mind the floor. I can sleep in the shop, if you prefer," he suggested.

"That would be absurd. I should be the one to sleep in the shop," she argued.

"If that's what you wish," he said, but she could see that the suggestion pained him.

"I must pay you back for your hospitality. I don't know how, though, as I don't have a job anymore. Would you let me help you with your work until I get a job somewhere else?"

He shook his head. "Don't go somewhere else. Please, stay. I need help in the shop. There's enough work for two at the moment, and even if there wasn't...Please, don't go."

Grazia was confused by his pleading. "Why are you doing this for me? I was rude to you when we met, and I've brought you nothing but trouble."

He opened his mouth to speak but thought better of it and closed it again.

Georgia walked in, eating bruschetta. "Grazia, I thought you were at the deli. Your mum is giving away complimentary bruschetta. It's delicious," she said, biting into the tomato-topped bread.

"My mother and I are no longer talking to each other."

As Grazia said the words, she waited for the pain that would come with it, but there was none. There was only liberation and release.

"I hope she's managing on her own."

"She's not on her own. Rupert, the antiques dealer, is helping her. They seem to have everything under control, so don't worry," Georgia told Grazia.

Rosaria didn't need her anymore, then. She had replaced her with Rupert. Grazia hadn't lost Rosaria's love because there had never been any. Now she was free.

"Thank you," Grazia said.

Hector squeezed her hand under the counter.

They finished her dress and she

tried it on in the same changing room where she had tried it the first time.

When he asked her to stand on the stool and walked around her, checking every crease and fold of the dress, she sensed she wasn't the only one finding the attention personal and unsettling in a delicious way.

That first time, when he had smoothed the fabric over her hips, his fingers had been still and confident. This time his fingers quivered and skimmed the fabric as if they feared touching her. This wasn't the touch of a professional anymore. They had become friends.

"I think we should take it in a little here." He pointed to her waist, asking for permission to move the pin.

"Yes, do," she said.

Only then did he pinch the fabric over her body and move the pin.

She took off the dress, he finished the last seams and she tried it on one last time.

"Thank you. It fits me perfectly!"

"Now you're ready to meet The One," he said with a smile that didn't reach his eyes.

"Yes, ready to meet The One."

She knew her own smile hadn't reached her eyes either.

Rebecca was in Calais, ready to board a ferry that would take her home. Her wedding dress was ready for tomorrow and Grazia's dress was ready too. The trouble was that Grazia didn't want to meet The One at the wedding anymore. Because she had fallen in love.

Hector Gonzales wasn't how she had imagined The One would be, and his surname wasn't any more British than her own. She didn't care, though. She had fallen in love.

Blending in and fitting in didn't matter. What mattered was fitting into the heart of the people she loved.

Even if Hector would never be in love with her romantically, he had fitted her into his heart. He had welcomed her into his home, his shop and his life.

CHAPTER 40

Grazia's phone rang, providing a welcome distraction.

Automatically she though it would be Rosaria, scolding her for being late to help her at the deli. Thankfully that would not happen again.

It was Rebecca.

"Hello! How are things? Are you on

the ferry?"

"Not good. I'm not on the ferry," her friend said, but the cheerfulness in her voice was evident. "I'm still in Calais. I had a ticket to get across but I've just given it to somebody who needed it more."

"How could they need it more than a bride trying to get to her wedding?" Grazia asked in disbelief.

There was a pause at the other end. "Well, you see, this bride isn't trying to get to her wedding anymore."

Her friend must have lost her mind!

"Are you all right, Rebecca?"

"Perfectly! The thing is that, during this trip, I realised that I don't want to marry Charles anymore. So there's not going to be any wedding tomorrow after all. I'm sorry for messing up everyone's plans."

Grazia was still standing on the tailoring stool. She reeled and Hector offered her his arm. She stepped down and sat on the stool.

"Let me understand this—"

"I'm sorry, Grazia, but I'm also not sorry at all. I'm the happiest I've been in a long time."

"So Charles wasn't The One?" Grazia asked.

"I never thought he was. It was a marriage of convenience. We were both afraid of spending our old age on our own, but we were not in love," Rebecca explained.

"It's lucky you found out before you married him. How has Charles taken it?"

"He's not heartbroken. As I said, it was a marriage of convenience. He'll find someone else. All he was preoccupied about was the refunds on the wedding venue, photographer and so on. We've sorted all that."

"Will you get your money back?"

"Not exactly. I'll explain later."

"We have your wedding dress. Would you like me to try and return it to the shop?"

"No, thank you."

"I'd advise against keeping it for your sons' future brides."

"No, I wasn't thinking of that. I'll tell you more when I get back. I'm sorry if I've missed the opening of your deli."

Now it was Grazia's turn to smile. "I'll have to update you on the deli when you get back."

They ended the call and Grazia turned to Hector, who had been standing next to her all this time. "I think you might have heard that the wedding is off."

"Yes. How are you feeling about it? What are you going to do about meeting The One?"

"I'm a little shaken, of course. Charles is excellent husband material," Grazia replied. "But, no, I don't need to look for The One anymore."

She lifted her gaze up to him hopefully.

"I see," was all he said.

Her declaration of love died in her throat. If he so clearly wasn't rejoicing, there was no hope that he was romantically interested in her.

"Right, then, now we can put away all this wedding stuff and start working on your clients' suits," she declared.

CHAPTER 41

"After all my warnings, now bear in mind

That love defies checklists, because love is blind."

—From The Sicilian Mama's "How to Pick a Husband" blog.

Grazia woke up in Hector's bed again. He had insisted on

giving her his bedroom and, as his daughters had sided up with him, she had been outnumbered.

He'd made space for her things in his cupboard. Hanging her clothes next to his trousers and jackets had made her feel like a lover moving in. Only she wasn't. They were friends. When he needed something from his room, he waited until she had vacated it.

Today Rebecca should have been married. Grazia and Hector spent the morning in the shop, receiving clients. While Hector took their measurements, Grazia basted, darned and sewed by hand and on the machines.

At eleven o'clock Grazia remembered that Rebecca would have been walking down the aisle. At twelve-thirty everyone would have been sitting down to a meal. But none of these thoughts made her sad. The One was smoke and mirrors. This man at the overlocker machine was solid. Even if he wasn't hers.

At one minute to closing time, when the "Closed" sign was already turned and Hector was getting the keys to lock the door, Lord Oldwell strutted into the shop, throwing his stick about as well as his weight, as usual.

"We're about to close," Hector told him politely but firmly.

"You can spare half an hour for a new project of mine," the man argued.

"Actually, we can't," Hector told him.

"We?" Lord Oldwell looked around, his gaze skimming over Grazia at the till as if she were invisible.

"My assistant and I are closing. If you please, I'll see you on Monday." Hector held the door open for him.

Lord Oldwell looked as if he couldn't quite believe what he was hearing. "Young man, you must be feeling unwell. I'm here to commission a new handmade suit, if that wasn't clear."

"The matter can wait till Monday," Hector repeated unflinchingly.

Lord Oldwell scowled. "I see. Well, there will be no new suit for you. I'll take my custom elsewhere!" he shouted, marching out of the door.

Hector's face didn't betray emotion. "It's your choice. Enjoy the weekend," he said, locking the door behind the old man.

"I'm so proud of you!" Grazia cried. "I'm just sorry you've lost a commission."

"Don't be. Lord Oldwell is quick to order and slow to pay. He still owes me for the last suit I made for him. I wasn't going to take any more work from him until he paid up."

They counted the money in the till, locked up and climbed the stairs to the flat they now shared.

Rebecca had promised to come and see her as soon as she got back to Calcotbury. Grazia told her not to look for her at Rosaria's, but to come over to Hector's. Thankfully, Rebecca hadn't asked questions.

Grazia insisted on cooking dinner even if she hadn't yet been added to the family's cooking roster. Neither Hector nor the girls complained, and Grazia was pleased when they relished the pasta alla Norma she had cooked with aubergines and tomatoes.

CHAPTER 42

A little after seven, the doorbell rang.

"It's Rebecca!" Grazia leaped to her feet and rushed downstairs to the front door.

She flung the door open and there was Rebecca, looking bedraggled but happy. Behind her stood a handsome young man with a pair of sunglasses propped on his head, Italian style.

"Hello," Grazia said cautiously.

"Hello, sweetheart! This is Stefano," Rebecca said, beaming.

"Nice to meet you," he said in Italian, offering his hand to Grazia.

Grazia shook his hand without a word. Too many questions whirred in her head to select which one to articulate first.

"Can we come in?" Rebecca asked.

"Yes," Grazia said, unused to being in the position of host in Hector's home.

They followed her up the stairs and

into the sitting room where Hector's girls were gathered. It transpired that Rebecca hadn't given her boys any more details than Grazia.

A moment later, no doubt having been messaged by the girls, Rebecca's boys arrived too. Stefano was introduced to them, again without explanation.

While the sofa groaned under the weight of the teenagers perched on it, Hector and Grazia rushed to gather chairs and stools, and the kettle was turned on.

Everyone's eyes kept darting to the attractive Italian who was, despite his slender figure, the elephant in the room.

When each had a cup of tea or coffee, Rebecca began to speak.

"Stefano and I met at the airport's car rental desk. We were both desperate to get back to the UK and ready to use any means, fair or unfair, to secure a vehicle. Basically, we would have gouged each other's eyes out for a car!"

"Speak for yourself," Stefano said with a mock-offended smile.

"He was in front of me in the queue, but I had booked a vehicle online."

"So had I," Stefano put in.

Rebecca waved a dismissive hand. "That's of no consequence. There hadn't been enough returns to fulfil new bookings so we were both without a car. As we were both going to the UK, the lady at the desk suggested that we shared one car that had just been returned. Stefano wasn't so sure."

"Neither were you! And you were trying to imply that the car should have gone to you, even though I was before you in the queue," he argued, interrupting her.

Grazia liked the way they

interacted, each holding their own with humour.

"In the end we agreed to share," Rebecca finished.

"You've been travelling together all this way?" Grazia asked.

"Yes."

"Why didn't you tell us?"

"I thought you'd be alarmed if you knew that I was travelling with a stranger. I mean, look at him!" Rebecca joked.

There was clearly a camaraderie between them, but this still didn't explain why he was here with Rebecca instead of continuing his journey to his destination.

"Once I had decided to keep him a secret, I couldn't go back on it. Now I wish I had told you about Stefano from the very beginning—because it's going to come to you as a shock that we're getting married."

Grazia spat her tea onto her skirt. Around her, eyes goggled, eyebrows rose and jaws dropped.

"I know it sounds crazy. We've only just met and I'm older than Stefano by some years," Rebecca admitted. "But this trip has pulled us together in ways you couldn't imagine. We've got to know each other very well

—and we've fallen in love." Rebecca turned to Stefano and the look they exchanged confirmed her words.

"We've rescheduled the venue, the photographer and the catering, and we're getting married next month!" Rebecca told them, beaming at Stefano, who squeezed her hand.

So that was why Rebecca had been vague about the caterers' refunds and had asked Grazia to hold on to the wedding dress!

The news was a shock and Grazia was still reeling from it, but the couple looked so happy together that she was happy for them too.

"Time to celebrate!" Hector declared, extracting a bottle of bubbly from the back of a cupboard.

They toasted and cheered. George walked over to Stefano and struck up a conversation. Grazia crossed her fingers for George that he might be happy with this new choice of stepfather.

She served Stefano and Rebecca her leftover pasta alla Norma and then cleared their plates away.

CHAPTER 43

Finally Rebecca, Stefano and the boys made a move to go home.

"Would you like a lift back to your flat?" Rebecca asked Grazia.

She had forgotten that she hadn't given her news to her friend yet. She swallowed and braced herself for Rebecca's reaction. Would she look shocked, concerned, disapproving?

"I'm not going back to that flat. I don't live with Rosaria anymore. We had a big argument, I walked out and she disowned me."

A grin spread across Rebecca's face. "It was high time! I'm so glad you've finally seen sense—that relationship was toxic for both of you. Her fear of loneliness made her hold on to you in a suffocating way and didn't allow either of you to live happy lives."

Was it true? It wasn't just her who was happier without Rosaria, but Rosaria was happier and healthier without her too? The thought wiped the last traces of guilt from Grazia's heart.

"Do you need a place to stay?" Rebecca wanted to know.

Grazia hesitated and felt her cheeks warm up at the thought of admitting to her friend that she was living in this small flat with this kind man and his daughters. That they were only friends, but he had given her his bed and slept on the floor of his daughters' room.

Rebecca must have put two and two together because her hands flew to her mouth.

"Oh, my! You're staying with Hector, of course!" she cried with such exultation that it made Grazia's cheeks heat up even more.

"It's not what you think, Rebecca. He's my boss. I work for him and the job comes with lodgings," she explained lamely.

Rebecca smiled knowingly. "And where exactly are your 'lodgings'?"

If Grazia told Rebecca that she was sleeping in Hector's room, it would confirm her friend's suspicions so she stayed quiet.

Rebecca laughed. "You don't have to tell me. Congratulations, sweetheart. You have waited so long and now you've finally met a thoroughly good man. He'll make you very happy," she added.

"We're only friends," Grazia corrected her, trying not to sound sad about it.

"A moment ago he was only your employer, yet now you're friends? I think this is a promising trend."

Rebecca was already on her way downstairs, calling over her shoulder that they should catch up again tomorrow.

Grazia didn't join the others saying their goodbyes downstairs. Instead, she busied herself collecting mugs and plates and tidying the kitchen.

Rebecca's words had wrapped her in melancholy and longing for this man who was so near to her and still so far. She slept in his bed, lived in his house, cooked for his family and worked in his shop, yet he would never think of her as more than a friend.

She turned off the tap and started drying the dishes on the drying rack. There was a rumble of steps up the stairs, and the bubbly voices of the girls intertwined with the low tones of their father's voice.

CHAPTER 44

Someone stopped in the corridor, just outside the kitchen.

"You can't pine for Mum forever." It was Ella's voice.

"It's not about your mum." His deep baritone was unmistakeable.

Grazia stopped drying the plate

and held her breath.

"What is it, then?" Ella asked.

"Grazia," he said.

"Don't you like her?" Ella asked.

Grazia's knuckles went white around the plate she was holding. Did she want to hear Hector's answer? Perhaps she should start singing loudly, or burst out of the room.

She didn't, she held her breath and continued listening.

"God knows how much I like her!"

Grazia's knees buckled under her and she reeled against the counter, still holding the plate by a miracle.

"Then what's the problem?" Ella

asked.

"If I ask her out when she's living under my roof and working in my shop, she won't be free to turn me down. It would be unfair to put her in that situation," he finished.

He was even more of a gentleman than she had thought.

"But I think she likes you, Dad."

Grazia nodded vigorously.

"As friend, yes. As a husband, no. She made it clear that she's looking for a particular kind of man and I'm not it."

"What kind of man?"

"The other day, she said that

Rebecca's ex-fiancé, Charles, was perfect husband material and that she didn't need to look for The One anymore," Hector growled.

Grazia's jaw dropped. No, no, no, he had got it wrong! She loved Hector —he was The One!

The person she had imagined didn't exist. It was an impossible, unreachable myth she had created to protect herself. Perhaps because the more unreachable he was, the more unlikely she was ever to meet him and be hurt by his rejection. She had never believed that a good man would be interested in her.

Hector was even better than that: he was the man she loved.

"I see," Ella said. "I can understand her saying that. Charles is rich and powerful. That's stiff competition for you."

Grazia wanted to shout, but couldn't because her body had frozen.

"I know. Off you go and get ready for bed so I can go to bed too," Hector ordered.

Still frozen to the sink, Grazia heard familiar steps trudge into the kitchen.

"Hello!" Hector sounded surprised.

"You didn't have to wash up. We can do it tomorrow with everyone's help."

She couldn't turn around or even speak.

"Are you okay?" he asked, coming up behind her and looking round at her.

His eyes were the colour of the sea in Sicily.

He must have seen the tears running helplessly down her cheeks.

"Oh, no! Sweetheart, what's wrong?"

She still couldn't speak, so he gathered her into a hug that melted the last little bit of her heart. She burst into sobs of relief and happiness.

One of the girls must have heard her because a hand closed the kitchen door, giving them privacy.

He stroked her hair, still holding her.

"Are you upset about your friend's wedding being called off? Are you feeling sorry for Charles?"

She opened her mouth to speak, but only sobs came out.

"Is it about Rosaria? Did Rebecca say something about her?" he asked.

All Grazia could do was shake her

head.

He took in a sharp breath. “You heard me in the corridor, didn’t you?”

She nodded and looked up into his very blue eyes.

“I’m an idiot—I shouldn’t have spoken there. Now you’ll feel uneasy about staying here and working with me. I’ve put you precisely in the situation where I didn’t want you to be. Please forget what I said,” he pleaded.

Grazia shook her head and tears rolled down her cheeks.

“I can’t do that, Hector,” she croaked between tears, “because I’ve fallen in love with you!"

The smile that spread across his face was as beautiful as a sunrise. "You love me?"

He was looking at her with marvel and joy, in a way nobody had ever looked at her in her whole life.

She nodded vigorously, dislodging more tears, and Hector bent down and kissed her.

EPILOGUE

The tailor of Calcotbury was always closed on a Sunday, but he and his fiancée were at work in the shop.

They were expecting a delivery of white silk satin, and they were measuring, planning and drawing.

"I'm still not sure that a groom

should be making his bride's wedding dress," Grazia Colonna, soon-to-be Gonzales, said.

"That's why I'm only making the pieces. You'll put them together."

Grazia's sewing skills had improved since she had started helping in the workshop. Now, if she wanted to let out the seams of one of her dresses, she wouldn't hesitate to do it herself.

But she was thankful that this hadn't been the case when she'd first set foot in Hector's shop.

Soon Hector would stop sleeping in his daughters' bedroom and would join her in the double bed.

Rosaria's Pantry, now also a coffee shop, was doing roaring business. This was thanks in part to Rupert, who sent customers over for a beverage when their resolve to buy eye-wateringly expensive antiques faltered.

These days Rosaria was too happy to hold grudges and went as far as greeting Grazia if they met in the street.

Grazia attended Rebecca's wedding with Hector and his daughters. It dawned on Grazia that, if she hadn't met Hector before, she would have met him at Rebecca's wedding. Her hunch about meeting The One there hadn't been wrong, in fact.

Ella still followed the Sicilian Mama's "How to Pick a Husband" blog eagerly. Grazia kept this in mind when she wrote a new post under the name of her online persona.

For years the Sicilian Mama had dispensed the wise, loving advice that Grazia had longed to receive from Rosaria. Writing the blog had been Grazia's way of encouraging herself and others.

Now she felt it was time to wrap it

up. Some time in the future she might start a new blog—perhaps about how to have happy, healthy marriages.

Love can come early or it can come late,

But don't lose faith: search and wait.

Never despair because there are cases

Where love shows up in unexpected places.

Keep your eyes peeled and your heart

Warm and running and ready to start.

This is Sicilian Mama's last post,

above,

Because she, too, has found love.

Love requires attention and time

And now I need to devote mine

To the one who makes my heart sing

And turns my winter into spring.

The End

ABOUT ME

Hello, I'm Stefania Hartley and I write heartwarming and humorous stories about down-to-earth, relatable characters.

Some of my stories are set in Sicily, where I grew up. Others are set in Singapore, were I've lived for a few years. The rest are set in England, where I live now in a small town like the one in "Tales from the Parish".

When I'm not writing or looking after the family, I'm reading, walking

or tending to my vegetable garden.

I love hearing from readers, so please do get in touch through my website or sign up for my newsletter at: www.stefaniahartley.com

And if you've enjoyed this story, please, leave a review :-)

OTHER BOOKS BY STEFANIA HARTLEY

Second Chances at

Mamma's Trattoria

Sweet Competition for

Camillo's Café

The Italian Fake Date

Under Far Eastern Skies

Good Habits

Welcome to Quayside

Tales from the Parish

Sand, Sea & Tamburello

To Be Loved

Keeping It Cool

A Slip of the Tongue

A Season of Goodwill

Stars Are Silver

Drive Me Crazy

What's Yours is Mine

Confetti and Lemon Blossom

Fresh from the Sea

Father Roberto and

the Runaway Ring

Father Roberto and the

Missing Money

Father Roberto and the Rural Riots

Printed in Dunstable, United Kingdom

67486510R00241